FIGHT [...]!

Suddenly his horse swung his head to look down the ravine, ears pointed. Mason flicked his gaze past the fire. Three men in western garb stealthily approached, staying pretty well bunched together. Mason realized that they could see into the shelter and view the fire. They were obviously puzzled when they saw no one bedded down close to it. They were warned now. Mason stood.

"Hands clear of your holsters and you won't get hurt," Mason said.

One of them made a move for his gun. Mason fired. There were only two to worry about now . . .

*   *   *

SPECIAL PREVIEW!

Turn to the back of this book for a sneak-peek excerpt from the exciting, brand-new Western Series . . .

FURY

. . . the blazing story of a gunfighting legend.

TOMAHAWK CANYON

JACK BALLAS

JOVE BOOKS, NEW YORK

TOMAHAWK CANYON

A Jove Book / published by arrangement with
the author

PRINTING HISTORY
Jove edition / July 1992

ISBN: 0-515-10879-0

Jove Books are published by The Berkley Publishing Group,
200 Madison Avenue, New York, New York 10016.
The name "JOVE" and the "J" logo
are trademarks belonging to Jove Publications, Inc.

PRINTED IN THE UNITED STATES OF AMERICA

10 9 8 7 6 5 4 3 2 1

To Harriette, my wife,
for making all my trails shady and down hill,

and to the DFW Writers Workshop
for smoothing the way.

TOMAHAWK CANYON

1

COLE MASON REINED in his horse, well back from the edge of the rimrock. He stepped from the saddle and patted the horse's strong black neck. "Stand easy, old friend. I'm gonna take a look-see. That town we heard about ought to be in that basin ahead."

It was early fall, 1879. Mason was in the middle of Jicarillo Apache country, Northern New Mexico Territory. The majority of the Apaches were contained on their reservation near Chama, but there were still renegades who jumped out on their own and raided isolated ranches. Earlier in the day Mason had spotted tracks of unshod ponies. He had faults, but no one could ever accuse him of being careless.

Dropping flat onto the rocky ground, he slithered toward the rim. It was said that Cole Mason could out-Indian an Indian when it came to tracking and moving without sound, though Mason had seen a lot of Indians against whom he'd not try to prove the truth of that statement.

Reaching a point where he could scan the basin below, he took his hat off and placed it beside his leg, not wanting to skyline more of himself than necessary.

Raising his head very slowly, Mason peered over. Spread below was ranch country as he had only dreamed existed. The grass was as deep as a horse's belly, with plenty of water. A creek ran there, meandering through the heart of the valley, fed by dozens of smaller streams. In the Big Bend they'd call that creek a river, Mason thought.

The vastness of the rolling landscape was broken by clumps of trees, aspen that would afford cattle some protection from wind and snow.

Cole's father, Brad Mason, had told him to try and find land

1

with good grass and water on his way home from delivering the herd to Montana.

He'd found it and now he hoped it was for sale. Mason couldn't quite believe such a place really existed.

Feeling the tug of his tied-down holsters pulling at his thighs, he frowned and looked at the two .44s hanging there. If only, he thought, I could spend a little time in this valley without somebody recognizing me. Not likely to happen, though. In a town of this size, it seemed there was always someone looking for trouble.

About eight miles south he saw a cluster of gray, unpainted buildings. He took them to be the town of Rock Creek, and the valley he looked upon would be Rock Creek Valley. He saw that it was not much of a town. A fast count showed only twelve buildings, but at that this was more than he'd seen in some time. He felt a need to see people, and that town, regardless of its size, promised to fulfill his need.

His gaze swept the rest of the basin. He saw nothing of interest. Mason placed his hands to push back from the rim when he saw a lone horseman emerge from a small clump of trees about a quarter of a mile from the bottom of the escarpment to his left. It looked as though the rider also had his sights set on the town. Mason figured to intercept him and have company the last few miles.

He inched back toward his horse. Just because he saw nothing but the one rider didn't mean there was no one else. This was Apache country—and an Apache let you see him only when he wanted to be seen.

Far enough back so as not to be skylined, Mason stood and put on his hat, then pulled his sheepskin coat tighter around his shoulders. It was getting colder. A glance at the leaden sky confirmed his estimate of earlier in the day. "Looks like it might snow," he grunted, picked up the trailing reins and mounting. "All right, horse, let's find us a way down into that valley." He had never gotten around to naming his horse.

He had ridden maybe a half-mile when he crossed an old game trail, and though long out of use, it was one he thought might get him to the bottom. Mason followed it to the edge of the rim and urged the black down the steep slope.

The black horse had run wild until three years before, and Mason had chased him down slopes as steep as this one before getting his rope around the stout black neck. This time he was lucky; his horse found the way to the bottom without having to backtrack.

Upon reaching level ground, Mason glanced to see that the rider was about a half-mile away now. Mason set a course that would intercept him.

The black waded through stirrup-deep grass. Looking at it, Mason thought of his father. He had not seen him or the home ranch in over six months, and he felt a sudden urge to see familiar people and territory. Pa wouldn't believe grass like this unless he saw it, Mason thought.

A flicker in the corner of his eye broke his thoughts. He looked where he'd seen movement and saw them come over the brow of a hill behind the horseman. He knew them for an Apache war party; they were controlling their mounts with their knees while holding their rifles with both hands. The rider had not seen them, and now the Apaches were closing fast, running their horses all out.

There were eight of them by Mason's count. Through narrowed lids he studied the rider and figured him for a boy; he was too small for a man.

Without thought he urged his horse into a run, something the big horse knew well. He seemed to fly across the tall grass as Mason dragged his Winchester from its scabbard.

He was about fifty yards to the side and behind, when the rider looked back. He could see now that the rider was a girl, from the length of auburn hair streaming in the wind behind her. Mason held his rifle at arm's length, pointing toward the Apaches, whose horses were running belly to the ground.

The girl looked in the direction he was pointing and simultaneously dug heels into her horse. Mason drew abreast with ease, but at the same time realized it would be futile to try to outrun the Apaches, who obviously could smell victory against such a small party. They fired sporadically, their shots not coming close enough to worry Mason—at least not yet.

There was a swale to his left, and Mason reined toward it, the girl following. He pulled on the reins, dragging the black to a halt. Before his horse stopped, Mason left the saddle running and slapped the black on the rump, urging him toward the creek about fifty yards away. The black would stay close to water until Mason called or came for him.

Mason threw himself flat, just below the swell of ground. The girl landed beside him, her rifle already belching fire. Mason's quick glance showed him a petite, green-eyed beauty, auburn hair windblown about her face as she stared in the direction of the oncoming Apaches.

"Hold your fire until you can draw a good bead," he shouted.

Now that the war party had lost the advantage of surprise, they dropped from their horses into the tall grass. Mason knew that it would now be a waiting game, but he was a patient man. He'd seen many a man in a hurry die for it.

The wind picked up, and he felt a drop of rain on the back of his neck. "Looks like we're gonna have a long, wet night, youngster. Watch the tops of the grass; you'll be able to tell any movement they make."

He took his eyes off the grass long enough to again flick a glance at the small figure beside him, almost hidden inside her own sheepskin, hat pulled low over her face. "You ever tangle with the Apache before?" Mason asked.

She shook her head.

"All right, just remember, do what I tell you, and if I say move, do it fast. Right now we've got to wait them out. When they get close they'll rush us."

The cold rain was falling in earnest now. Mason saw the tops of the grass bend toward him, in four different places, and pointed them out to the girl.

Then they came. Mason fired twice, as fast as he could lever shells into the chamber, and saw red blossom on the chests of two of the warriors. Then a third had blood spurting from a neck wound. The girl had gotten that one. Her rifle was singing its own tune. The Apaches dropped back into the grass, out of sight, minus three who wouldn't be doing any more fighting today.

"Five to go," Mason grunted. "Turn around, easy now, and watch our rear." Then almost as an afterthought, he added, "Good shooting, young lady."

He could not see the downed Apaches in the tall grass. The others had probably already dragged them off. An Indian never left his dead on the field of battle if he could help it.

A trickle of rain between his shoulder blades caused Mason to shiver and pull down tighter into his sheepskin. It was then, that he saw the grass about fifty yards out bend against the wind.

He fired where he gauged the Indian to be and, in the almost dead quiet, heard a faint but solid thump of lead into flesh. He saw a warrior stand, claw at his chest, and fall.

About ten minutes dragged by; then at a distance Mason saw the remaining Apaches riding off, their dead slung across the backs of ponies. From past experience he knew they were not afraid; they just didn't like the odds and would try again— but not today.

He rolled to his feet with one fluid move. "All right, young lady, they're gone. Let's head for town."

"Don't call me young lady," his companion said, whipping off the flat-crowned, wide-brimmed hat. "I'm a full-grown woman, almost as old as you."

Mason looked at her, raising an eyebrow. "Well, so you are."

"Nineteen makes most women grown, I hear tell."

"Yep, and you're the most nasty tempered grown woman I've ever seen," he said, ignoring her sarcasm. His look took in the long auburn hair tumbling in disarray down her back. The rough man's garb did little to hide the soft curves filling her shirt. Despite his words, Mason had never seen a woman who made him want to shelter and protect her more than this petite bundle of dynamite.

"Sorry, ma'am. I reckon I just didn't take time to notice," he continued. "I go by the name of Mason, Cole Mason."

She stood there, head tilted, looking at him. "Humph, you're like all men, like a cow, don't see anything beyond the end of your nose. Because I'm short you figured I was a kid." Acid still dripped from her words, but then of a sudden her face softened and chagrin marked the corners of her mouth. "I'm sorry, Mr. Mason. I reckon I felt the need to blow off at something after all this." Then sticking out her hand, she said, "Laura Bryson. Thanks for getting me out of trouble. I left our ranch up north of here this morning. Papa is looking to meet me in town." She frowned. "I knew there were renegade Jicarillos on the prowl, but didn't hear of any in these parts. I thought they were all on the reservation, a hundred miles northwest."

Mason glanced toward the departing Apaches. "Well now,

ma'am, I reckon we both know better."

He looked toward the creek. "You sit tight. I'll gather up our horses. We'd better get you on into town."

In the time it took for them to ride to town, the rain stopped, and the lowering clouds blanked out any remaining daylight.

They drew rein in front of the Cattleman's Hotel. The golden glow of lantern light from the windows looked especially inviting after the cold, wet ride. Mason stepped down, circled his horse's rump, and reached up to help Laura down. "You go on in and find your pa. I'll stable the horses."

"He'll want to thank you when he gets a chance," Laura said.

Mason nodded, and walked toward the livery.

The black light-stepped through the open door of the stable. Mason stepped from the saddle and loosened the cinches on both horses.

He felt the old man in the livery stable watching with approval as he took care of both horses before asking that they be given grain.

The liveryman looked at the Circle B brand on Laura's horse, then shifted his gaze to the B-bar-M on the rump of Mason's. The old man turned to Mason. "You're new around here. Riding for the Bryson brand?"

"No," Mason said, knowing the old man wanted to ask more, but wouldn't. People were careful of the questions they asked out here, so Mason volunteered more information. "Miss Bryson and I met up outside of town a piece and rode in together."

He'd thought of leaving the telling of the Apache incident to Laura, but he knew that the safety of too many people depended on it. He told the liveryman what had transpired. Between Laura and the liveryman the story would spread.

The old man's eyes shifted to look at Mason's tied-down holsters. He started to say something, then apparently changed his mind.

"It'll be fifty cents a day for grain, fresh hay, and a clean stall. Pay me when you leave." He turned away and rubbed his palms down his trousers.

The old man hesitated, then pointed at the guns against Mason's thighs. "Mister, you seem like a decent sort. If you can use them guns, the Circle B needs a friend."

"Thanks, old-timer, but seems to me like they already have one." Mason was curious as to the nature of Bryson's trouble, but the old man had already turned away and was forking hay into the black's stall. Mason had been dismissed. He headed toward the hotel, but then went into the saloon instead. A drink, after being wet and cold, would warm his gut.

A glance inside the saloon showed the typical large room cluttered with tables. There were more people—sitting around talking, drinking, and playing cards—than Mason would have expected on a night like this. Mostly town people, he judged by their clothing and unweathered complexions.

The room was warmed by large potbellied stoves at each end. The bar spanned the length of the wall adjacent to the hotel. Mason was surprised to see that it was made of beautifully finished hardwood, hand-rubbed and oiled, a fine furnishing for this remote area.

A look showed the bartender to be the big redheaded side of beef resting his elbows on the counter. At the same time, Mason noticed three punchers, drunk and rowdy, but he thought, Hell, after a few weeks of nothing but cows, they deserved to blow off steam.

He found a place at the bar, and got the bartender's attention. He pointed his finger toward the shelf under the bar. "Give me some of your private stuff. Bourbon, if you have any."

"Cost you twice as much," the bartender said, "but if that's what you want, you got it." He brought up a bottle of Kentucky's best and poured a liberal amount into a water glass.

Lifting the glass to his lips, Mason swallowed and felt the liquid warm his insides, driving some of the chill from his bones.

A hatchet-faced puncher, one of the rowdy ones he'd noticed earlier, sneered and said, "What's the matter, ya too good to drink whisky?"

Mason turned slowly, knowing what to expect. He'd been over this trail before. The puncher stood five feet away, primed for trouble.

Mason's words were soft so only those close by could hear. "Felt like something better tonight. Sit down and let it ride."

A cold glint came into the puncher's eyes, and Mason knew he'd made a mistake. This puncher was a gunhand looking to add to his reputation.

"What's the matter, you afraid?" It was obvious that he expected Mason to draw. No one west of the Mississippi took those words, except a coward or a man who had nothing to prove.

Mason had nothing to prove.

He grinned, stepped forward, and, with the swiftness of a striking rattlesnake, threw the contents of the glass in the gunman's face and fired his left fist in an uppercut that nearly tore the gunny's head off.

The puncher, surprise and hate flooding his face, hit the floor, and reached for his gun. He was too late. He was staring into the bore of Mason's .44.

"Finish that draw and I'll see if you'll bleed from a .44 hole in your gut," Mason said. "Now get up and walk over to the bar and order me some of that good bourbon under the counter." Mason's eyes were flat and deadly. "You spilt mine, so you're gonna buy me another."

Mason deliberately holstered his .44, daring this would-be badman to try his luck.

The young gunman said, "I'll buy you a drink . . . in hell."

The devil rode Mason's shoulders. He was angry clear through. He'd come in here wanting only a drink and maybe a little friendly talk before supper.

A glance showed Mason that the other two he'd seen with this young tough were standing clear, their hands held away from their holsters. "Now it's *two* drinks," he said.

His fist lashed out again, and for the second time in as many minutes, the gunman was knocked flat. "And every time I have to knock you down it's gonna be another. Make me happy and buy a round for the house."

He watched the gunny get slowly to his feet. A killing desire was in the man's eyes, but also doubt.

"Just put a gold eagle on the bar."

The gunman turned away. Almost by magic, Mason's .44 appeared. "Go ahead," he said, his voice harsh.

The gunman's eyes were pure poison, but he reached into his pocket and tossed a gold eagle on the bar.

"Pour me two of your best," Mason said over his shoulder, not taking his gaze off the reputation-hunting gunman. "And keep the change. The gentleman is feeling generous tonight."

One of the puncher's buddies said, "C'mon, let's get out

of here. You're lucky. You ne'er seen the day you could beat 'im."

"Bart can beat him," the puncher said. "Bart an' me'll run that slick gun out of town before daylight."

"C'mon, Tom, leave it."

Mason downed his drink, and motioned to the remaining one on the counter. "Have a drink, bartender. We just had a generous guest." He walked out before any more was said by Tom's friend, or the bartender. He didn't want trouble. All he wanted was a big steak and a warm bed.

When he stepped into the lobby the next morning he felt like a new man. A good night's sleep, a bath, and a shave had glazed over his trouble of the night before. As soon as he could wrap himself around a half dozen eggs, and some coffee, he'd be ready for the world.

Someone pushed through the front door, and Mason saw that the rain had changed to snow during the night. Nodding to himself, he thought that in this high country there was likely to be a lot before it quit; there were about six inches already.

Before entering the dining room, he stopped at the registration desk. A tall, gangling youth was sitting behind it and appeared to be trying to look busy.

He looked up. "Mawnin," he drawled, an infectious smile spreading across his homely face. "What can I do for you?"

Mason returned his smile. "I need some information," he said and described the events of the night before. "I like to know who my enemies are. Who braced me?"

"I heard all about it last night. They were Bart Slade's men. Tom—he's the one braced you—is Bart's brother. They're all hardcases. Run a ranch over east of here. You want to watch out for them."

The kid leaned toward Mason. "It's said Bart's faster'n Billy Bonney. You'll know him when you see him. He's tall . . . almost as tall as you although not as big in the shoulders. Got a scar runs from the corner of his right eye down to the corner of his mouth. Watch out for him. He's just as mean as he looks."

"Thanks. Now I think I'll surround some breakfast." He turned toward the dining room.

Finding a seat at the back of the room to his liking, Mason sat, with his back to the wall. He felt a twinge of disappointment that Laura wasn't around. He wondered why he missed that pocket-sized filly.

When the fried eggs, steak, potatoes, and biscuits had disappeared, Mason lingered over a second cup of coffee, then looked up expectantly as two people entered the room. He hoped it would be Laura, and again disappointment flooded him. It was Tom Slade and his brother Bart. The scarred face described by the kid at the desk was unmistakable. They pulled up to a table across the room.

Resentment welled up in Mason's gut. He had been enjoying the peace and quiet; now there would be trouble. He didn't doubt for a minute that the Slades would bring it.

Tom Slade leaned over, said something, and nodded toward Mason at the back of the room. Bart, poison mean from the look of him, glanced toward Mason, then looked back at his brother.

Mason quietly dropped his hand into his lap, eased it back to his holster, and drew his .44, letting it rest on his leg.

The Slades stood and walked over to him. Bart grimaced in what might have passed for a grin and stuck out his hand. "Name's Bart Slade. Hear you and my little brother had some trouble last night. Hope there's no hard feelings."

Mason wanted nothing to do with either Slade. He didn't take Bart's hand; to do so would have put his right hand out of business.

"No hard feelings." His words fell between them like lead slugs. "But you got it wrong. *We* didn't have any trouble last night. Your brother did."

Bart's hand dropped to his side.

"Don't get any ideas about that .44," Mason said. "Mine's trained for the middle of your belly."

With a smile that didn't reach his eyes, Bart said, "Well now, I like to see a man prepared. I run a spread over east of here. Could use a man with your talents. You looking for a job?"

Mason said, "Sorry, but I'm heading for Texas in a few days. Besides, I'm damned particular who I ride for. You're not even close." As he finished he saw the flicker in Bart's eyes again.

"Don't do anything foolish. Don't ever try lead slugs for breakfast." Mason shook his head, sadly. "Give a man an awful case of indigestion."

Their eyes venomous, the brothers turned and headed for the door. Bart stopped and said, "Mister, whoever you are, you just made the biggest mistake of your life." He stomped out.

Mason holstered his gun. He had made a bitter enemy. What the hell, he was heading for Texas as soon as the snow stopped.

He drank another cup of coffee, hoping Laura would come in. Aside from being a beautiful woman, she had a lot of spunk. Mason frowned, puzzled. He'd given few women a second thought.

Swallowing the last of his coffee, he pushed back from the table, thinking to walk down to the livery stable and check on his horse. That big black was the best he'd ever had.

He stepped out of the hotel door after carefully scanning the street, doorways and windows. He didn't really believe the Slades would drygulch him in the middle of town, but now was not the time to get careless.

It was snowing harder, which meant he would not be leaving as soon as planned. He headed for the livery at a fast clip. The wind was frigid and blowing harder, burning his lungs like fire.

He pushed open the stable door, slid through, and quickly closed it. At the black's stall, he saw that his horse had plenty of water and had been fed. "Looks like you're gonna get a pretty good rest, old horse." Mason chuckled as the black stuck his nose out and nuzzled him. "No, no, don't thank me. If it wasn't for this weather we'd be heading for home."

Turning, he walked to the room in the corner that served as an office and living quarters for the old man who ran the place. The potbellied stove, glowing cherry red, was a welcome sight.

The old man looked at Mason and pulled his pipe from his mouth. "Your hoss, he's been fed." He waved his pipe toward the door. "Seen your Texas rig. I came over here from Texas a few years back myself." He stuck out his hand. "Name's Jeb Murtry."

Mason gripped the gnarled old hand. "Cole Mason."

Murtry squinted at Mason. "Rode fer a brand down in the

Big Bend owned by Brad Mason. Mighty fine man. Any kin
o' yours?"

"You might say such. He's my pa."

"The hell you say," Murtry said. Then he admitted, "I s'pose
I oughtta tell you, I knowed you was off Brad's place by the
brand yore hoss is carryin'. Reckon you was away to that
there Army school at West Point whilst I rode fer yore daddy.
Knowed yore brother too. Clay's his name if I ain't fergot."

Mason grinned. "Reckon you haven't forgotten. Yep, Clay's
my brother."

Murtry's smile wrinkled his face like a drought-dried lake
bed. He said, "I shoulda knowed you was Brad's son. I
heard about last night. Yore pa woulda done the same thing.
Would've been proud a you, son." The grin faded to a frown.
"You better be real careful, boy. You done made yourself a
passel of enemies."

"Uh-huh, and I turpentined Bart Slade's ass this morning."
He went on to tell Murtry about the dining room fracas.

Murtry pursed his lips and blew a silent whistle. "Son, you
done it up right. Bart Slade's mean as a sidewinder, and strikes
about twice as quick."

"Then he's the reason Bryson needs a friend," Mason said.

"You done nailed that horseshoe down tight."

"I thought Bart Slade was down Lincoln County way, riding
with the Murphy-Dolan gang."

"Was, but he's here now, runnin' the same kinda game
Dolan's been runnin' down there. Runs a small spread. His
hands are mostly gunslingers. They get orders for Army beef,
round up any cows in sight and drive 'em off."

Murtry stopped talking to stoke his pipe and light it, then
said, "There ain't a rancher around here strong enough to
stand up to Bart Slade. He runs about fifteen hundred head,
but delivers three or four thousand, and don't ever draw the
count down on his own herd."

Mason stared thoughtfully at the wall, not seeing it. "Sounds
like one of two things: Dolan's spreading out, or Slade took
some mighty good lessons."

"Thing is, Mason, even with the money Slade's gettin' from
the cows he's selling, I don't reckon it'd be enough. He's got a
powerful lot of gunslingers on his payroll, and they don't come
cheap. Somebody else has to be in this with him."

"Old-timer," Mason said, "I'm headed home. If I wasn't, I think I would buy chips in this game." He glanced out the window. It was blowing up a blizzard. "I can't leave until this weather lets up, so, think I'll go back to the hotel and see if Miss Laura's in the dining room."

Murtry shook his head. "You won't be finding her there. She and her pa left out of here 'bout daybreak, headin' fer the ranch."

Worriedly, Mason glanced out the window again. "That means they've been gone about two hours, and that's a serious blizzard kickin' up out there. Is Bryson the kind of man who'd know what to do in weather like this?"

Murtry scratched his head. "Reckon most times I'd give you a yeah to that question, but this mornin' they left without no blankets or provisions. They ain't about to make it to the ranch in this weather in one day. It warn't snowin' like this when they left. Bryson ain't no tenderfoot, but I'd reckon right now, him an' Miss Laura's got big trouble."

Mason looked at Murtry. "How far is the Bryson spread from here?"

"Oh, reckon it'd be 'bout twenty miles, straight north."

Mason buttoned his coat. "Mr. Murtry, saddle my horse, throw some grub in a gunnysack, and if you've got a couple extra blankets tie them to the back of my saddle. I'm going to the hotel for my gear. That girl and her father could be in real trouble. Gonna see if I can find 'em."

He walked out and, within a few feet of the door, was swallowed in a blanket of white.

When he reached the bottom of the hotel stairs, his gear slung across his shoulders, the gangling youth behind the counter handed him a folded piece of paper.

"Mr. Bryson left this for you fore he left. I forgot it earlier when you was in."

Mason read the note. Bryson thanked him for what he'd done for Laura, and regretted that, due to the weather, he could not stay and meet him, but invited him out to the ranch.

Mason folded the note and put it in his pocket. "Guess maybe I'll accept that invitation."

2

WHEN MASON RETURNED to the stable, Murtry had saddled his horse, tied his bedroll on, and packed a gunnysack with food. Mason tossed a gold coin to Murtry. "In case I don't get back this way, this should cover my bill."

Murtry tossed it back. "I reckoned to run a tab on you. Figured you'd stick around awhile. Like I said, Mr. Bryson needs help."

Mason pushed his Winchester into the boot and swung aboard. "Sounds like you're trying to buy me a pack a trouble." He smiled, not feeling much humor. "Well, que sera, sera." He pulled the black around and rode out the door.

The cold bit into his lungs, taking his breath as he reined into the wind. Pulling his neckerchief up over his face and his black flat-brimmed hat down over his eyes, he walked the black to the edge of town. Even in this storm he had the uncomfortable feeling of eyes watching him.

Mason hunched further into his sheepskin. If the Slades wanted him bad enough to come out in this weather, let them, but Slades be damned—that girl and her father were likely to need help. The piercing, needle-like snow pellets reinforced his thought.

The sudden change in the weather, from autumn chill to brutal mid-winter cold, was hard on men and animals alike. It happened every few years, but always many people weren't prepared for it.

Looking down at the road, Mason knew it would be futile to try to follow tracks; the snow drifted too fast for that. The most he could count on would be an occasional track, or sign in the lee of a cutbank, or perhaps broken branches of bushes or trees.

Despite this reasoning, he kept his eyes on the trail, looking up occasionally to get his bearings, though he could see very little. He was making slow time. In a day, at this rate, he might make seven or eight miles.

Mason had spent most of his life outdoors, trapping, hunting, and fighting. Those who knew him counted him as the best, but even so, he was having a rough time of it. He was not worried for himself—it was the Brysons that caused concern.

He didn't know how much experience Laura's father had in trying to survive in the open, without provisions or proper clothing. And not knowing caused him to push harder. Of one thing he was sure—they would not have started out had it not appeared that the fairly decent weather would hold.

Four hours on the trail with nothing but blowing, drifting snow, and he'd seen sign only twice. Those two occasions assured him the Brysons were still ahead. He was counting heavily on his horse to tell him whether there was anybody close by.

It was a world of white, with no sound, no smell. He reined in, dismounted, and checked his horse. He cleaned the snow from around the frog inside the animal's steel shoes, and then checked his horse's nostrils for ice.

The black nuzzled him. Mason rubbed his ears and patted his neck, then swung back aboard. A good horse was often the difference between living or dying on some lonely trail. The black had been that difference for him many times.

Though riding into the wind was torture, it was in Mason's favor, the black would sense Bryson's party should Mason unknowingly pass within a few yards of them.

He depended more and more on the horse. It was getting late. He'd not seen sign for a couple of hours and was soon going to have to find a windfall, or any kind of shelter, and make camp. Maybe the next thicket of trees would be what he was looking for . . . and with luck, Laura and her father would have picked the same place.

It was when he made the decision to find shelter that he saw the black's ears prick and turn forward. The horse was looking straight ahead.

At the same time Mason caught a faint whiff of wood smoke. Relief flooded him. He wanted to hurry his horse and ride in, but he knew better than to do so.

With the Slades and Apaches on the prowl, he wanted to determine who'd be greeting him. He slipped to the ground, cupped his hand over the black's nostrils to keep him from announcing their presence, and closed in on the smoke smell. The snow seemed to be letting up.

A ravine angled toward the creek off to his right. The same stream, he knew, where he and Laura had stood off the Jicarillos. Mason dropped to his belly and wormed toward the lip of the ravine. Careful to expose no more of himself than necessary, he peered into its depths and saw a small fire flickering at the bottom. Two figures huddled close to its meager flame, one of them of slight build. He was almost sure it was Laura.

"Hello the fire," he yelled, his voice torn from his mouth by the icy bullwhip of the wind.

The two melted away from the fire, out of his line of sight.

"C'mon in, but keep your hands in sight," a male voice called out.

Mason retrieved his horse and held his .44 under his coat, not yet certain the people around the tiny fire were Laura and her father. Then, finding a gentle slope to the bottom, he approached the fire.

He recognized Laura immediately. She was huddled close to the fire, slightly under the overhang of the ravine. Even though he had met her only the day before, he'd have known that proud little figure anywhere.

"It's Cole Mason. C'mon out, Miss Laura."

She and a man Mason guessed to be in his mid-forties moved from under the lip of the ravine. The man held his rifle at the ready. If needed, that long gun would spit fire and lead in a second.

"What in the world are you doing out here?" Laura asked, through almost blue lips, her teeth chattering. Relief flooded her face.

"I heard that a *youngster* and her pa left town early, before this turned into a blizzard. Thought they might need help." He glanced at her to see if she would take the bait. She did.

She bristled, then relaxed with a grin and nodded. "You're right. A youngster talked her pa into trying to make it home in spite of his opinion that the storm was going to worsen." She looked at her father. "Pa, this is the man I told you about, Cole Mason."

"Looks like I owe you quite a debt, young man." Bryson stepped forward, his hand out. "I wanted to make your acquaintance in town this morning, but if we were going to make it to the ranch today, we had to get going."

Bryson looked toward the fire and grimaced. "Sorry I can't offer you anything to eat, or even a cup of coffee. We left town without provisions, figuring to get home before needing them."

"I got plenty here. We'll cook up some supper in a bit, but let's get a shelter fixed first."

"How?" Bryson looked around helplessly.

Mason picked up the few sticks of firewood stacked by the fire and put them on the flame. "You and Laura get in under the overhang and stay close to the fire. I'll fix a windbreak. Laura can start supper."

Mason stripped the gear off his horse and brought the gunnysack Murtry had packed to the fire. He handed it to Laura.

"There's coffee, bacon, and beans in there, some hard bread too. I'll rustle up firewood." He walked down the ravine toward the creek, knowing there would likely be wood there.

Returning to camp, Mason noted with approval that they'd done a good job of picking a place to stop. It was about as good as could be found to protect them from wind and cold, and he'd make it a lot better. Years of runoff had hollowed out a deep cut under the bank, almost forming a cave. He dropped his armload of wood and handed Laura a pot filled with snow for the coffee.

It was obvious she was no tenderfoot. She prepared the meal as though she did it every day under circumstances such as this.

Mason, with Bryson's help, gathered several more loads of wood. It was turning bitter cold. They would need every stick of it to keep from freezing.

Mason chopped five slender saplings and leaned them against the wall of the ravine. He cut boughs off a stand of cedar and wove them between the saplings until the mouth of the shallow cave was closed to wind and snow. Finally, he stepped back and looked for ways to make it better. Satisfied he'd done the best he could with what he had at hand, he went inside to eat.

After supper, with the fire blazing, Laura soon stopped shivering, and color returned to her face and lips.

Mason noticed Bryson, at sporadic intervals, cast quizzical glances in his direction, so he was not surprised when Bryson stoked his pipe and leaned toward him.

"Mason, I'm gonna lay my cards on the table, face up. You and your reputation are brought up at every camp fire in the West. I've never heard anyone say anything but good about you. Never heard of anyone willing to cross you neither."

He puffed life into his pipe, then asked bluntly, "You planning to join in this game here in the valley?"

Mason cocked an eyebrow. "Bryson, I never heard of this valley until yesterday. Didn't know anything was going on until this morning. Talked with Murtry at the livery."

He felt his face stiffen with anger. "I'm not playing. Slade offered me a job, but I told him I'm real choosy who I ride for." His pent-up anger bled into his voice. "I have a reputation. I didn't want it, but I got it. Never drew on any man unless he'd have it no other way."

Still angry, he continued, "I wouldn't know anything now except Murtry once rode for my pa down in the Big Bend. I was away at school, West Point."

He saw Laura shiver and pull down deeper into her sheep-skin. He stood, went to his bedroll, got his blanket, and put it around her shoulders.

"It's gonna be a long, cold night. You both get some sleep. I'll stand first watch."

Bryson said, "Watch? What are you gonna stand watch for? We're probably the only people crazy enough to be out in this weather."

Pulling his rifle from its scabbard, Mason squinted past the fire at Bryson. "Might be Apaches around." He walked beyond the rim of firelight.

He climbed out of the ravine. At the top the full blast of wind cut into him, but the snow had lightened. With no more cover than he had, an icy death would not be far away. Carefully he scanned all directions. Against the blanket of snow it was unlikely he'd miss any movement.

Already, his lungs burned, his hands and feet felt like lead weights. He returned to the fire, thinking to come up for a look every fifteen or twenty minutes.

Both Laura and her father slept huddled under his blanket, drawing warmth from each other.

Mason stared at them a moment, wondering why he was getting involved. A glance at Laura's sleeping form gave him his answer. It was a fool thing to do. He'd known this girl but one day.

He scanned the upper and lower ends of the ravine. His gaze flicked past the fire. Looking directly at it would blind him. No man who figured on a long life looked directly into a fire at night, especially in Indian country. Standing, he threw more wood on the fire. A big fire was dangerous, and could be more easily seen, but getting shot was no more final than freezing to death.

After two more trips to the top of the ravine, he'd still seen no movement. His eyes felt heavy. About ten more minutes and I'll wake Bryson, he thought. Suddenly, his horse swung his head to look down the ravine, ears pointed.

Avoiding the firelight, Mason crept to Bryson's side and placed his hand over the older man's mouth to stifle the usual groan that accompanied being woken for a night watch.

Bryson opened his eyes, obviously fully aware. Mason held his finger over his lips, signaling for quiet, then motioned for Bryson to get Laura in under the overhang as far as possible. He slipped back into the darkness.

Mason hunkered beside a large boulder across the narrow gulch, and watched both approaches to camp. He gave the down side most of his attention.

Knowing the Apaches did not like to fight at night, Mason discounted the possibility that they had Indians to contend with. He was right.

Three men in western garb stealthily approached the fire, staying pretty well bunched together. The confines of the ravine permitted small latitude for spreading out.

Mason realized that they could see into the shelter and view the fire. They were obviously puzzled when they saw no one bedded down close to it. They were warned now. Mason stood.

"Hands clear of holsters and you won't get hurt," he said.

One of them made a move for his gun. Mason fired, and then there were only two to worry about.

Bryson spoke from the darkness under the cutbank. "Don't be foolish and you might make it home."

The introduction of another party convinced the intruders. They held their hands well away from their holsters. Mason stepped into sight. It was just as he figured—Tom and Bart Slade glared at him across the fire.

Mason felt himself go quiet inside. "Go ahead." the softness of his voice belied the cold anger clutching his gut. "Reach for a gun. I'll fill my skunk limit." Mason knew they wouldn't try their luck.

Mason had to force himself to relax pressure on his trigger. The tension eased, and with it came a great letdown. He'd just killed one man and was ready to kill the other two. These men probably needed killing, but the anger had drained from him.

"Turn around." He motioned his gun in a circle. They turned, and Mason slipped their guns from their holsters, then threw them over by his saddle.

He glanced at Bryson out of the corner of his eye. "Get their horses." He looked back to the Slades. "You're lucky this time. Next time it'll be different. You're riling me a mite and that ain't healthy." He patted them down for knives or hideout guns and found none. "Now go," he said, and pointed toward the creek end of the ravine.

They started toward their horses.

"No," Mason said, "walk."

They faced him, astonishment registering across their faces. "Walk?" they asked at once. "We'll freeze to death out there."

Mason felt his eyes go flat and hard. "Next time you'll think before you come after me. If there wasn't a lady present you'd walk in blue skin—nothing 'tween it and fresh air." He motioned with his gun. "Go."

Bart's look was venomous. "When the time comes—you're mine."

"Can't wait." Mason's voice followed them out of the camp.

"It would have been kinder to shoot them," Laura said from across the fire. "Maybe you should have. They'll never let you live now—if they make it to their ranch without freezing to death."

Mason said, "I don't kill very easy." He saw belief in her eyes.

• • •

With the first gray of dawn the wind let up, and the snow slackened to flurries. Mason told Laura and her father he thought they could make it to the ranch if the drifts weren't too deep.

He tied the puncher he'd shot the night before to the saddle of one of the Slade horses and slapped the horse on the rump, saying, "Figure you won't get too ripe in this crisp air."

His eyes locked with Laura's. "Aren't you at all sorry you killed that man?" she asked.

Mason stared at her a long moment, then silently walked to his horse.

"Let's go home," Bryson said, echoing all of their sentiments.

Headed for the ranch, Bryson filled Mason in on the details of the valley situation as he saw it. It didn't sound good. Bryson shared the opinion Murtry had passed to Mason earlier: Someone else was involved in this, someone furnishing money.

Mason hooked a leg over his saddle horn and narrowed his eyes against the white glare.

"You know, it sounds like the second party is using Slade to rustle from the ranches, with money from the stolen cattle only partially paying for the gunhands. His final aim is probably to grab off all the land he can when the ranchers can't continue. They'd have to sell cheap, and the money-man's gonna end up with it all. Slade won't get anything."

Bryson nodded. "I think you're right." Looking toward a rise, he said, "Home is just over yonder a ways."

When they topped the rise, Mason saw that the ranch house and outbuildings were located so as to be functional, and were set at the base of a wooded slope that spoke of a man who loved beauty. The whole layout looked as solid and permanent as the mountain it snuggled against.

This creation of Bryson's gave Mason a glimpse into the soul of the man, and he liked what he saw. It was then he decided he just might buy chips in the game, but he would play by *his* rules.

As they dismounted in front of the house, Bryson asked Mason to stay in the main house as their guest. Mason declined. He wanted to stay in the bunkhouse with the hands to see the kind of men he was throwing in with.

Curt Tilghman, Bryson's foreman, walked with Mason from the main house. He was a tall, wiry man, not given much to talking.

He cast Mason a glance. "Hiring on?"

"Nope." Mason shook his head. "Name's Cole Mason. Thinkin' about staying around awhile though. You been with Bryson long?"

"Come out here with him, 'bout twenty-five years ago—him and his missus. After she died, Bryson and me raised Miss Laura. I showed her how to ride and shoot. She's right good at both." His eyes crinkled at the corners, which Mason thought might be as close as he ever got to an outright smile.

They pushed through the door of the bunkhouse.

"Throw your gear on any bunk that ain't got nothin' on it."

Mason found an empty bunk close to the potbellied stove and tossed his gear onto it. He unrolled his bedroll and made the bunk. After hanging his rifle from a post, he oiled and cleaned his .44.

Tilghman introduced him to the hands, eleven in all. Mostly, the introductions involved a meeting of the eyes and a nod; some prefaced the nod with a "Howdy." These men were not unfriendly—just reserved.

Mason, used to making quick judgments, liked these men right off. They were not salty fighting men like he'd known on his father's spread in the Big Bend country, but he figured they could fight when need be, and might be the type to stick with you.

Bob Brannigan was a different story. He was a slim, quiet young man who had been with Bryson three years. When Mason looked into his eyes, he read Brannigan as a man who would ride with you into the teeth of hell—if he was your friend.

Mason liked what he saw and would tell Bryson of his decision to stay. However, it wasn't until the next morning, at breakfast, that they talked.

Mason nodded his thanks as Laura poured him an after-breakfast cup of coffee, then said to Bryson, "I'm gonna stick around awhile—see what Slade's game really is."

"You want a job, you got it." Bryson sat back and puffed on his pipe. "Don't reckon I need to tell you I wanted you to stay right from the start. Hate to say it, but it's gonna come down to a fight in the end. I'm losing too many cattle, so are the others, and its gotten to the point now where we're gonna have to take down the tepee or fight. Reckon most of us'll fight."

Mason pursed his lips and nodded. "Figured you would, or I'd be heading for Texas right now."

He leaned across the table. "Bryson, don't put me on your payroll. I'll need free rein to come and go as I want. I don't want to feel obligated to do you a day's work, and I would if I took your money. Let me do it my way.

"I'll need a drawing of this valley. I plan to spend a lot of time in the saddle. When I get through I'll know every inch of your ranch, as well as the others."

Mason gazed into the bottom of his coffee cup, frowning. "I don't believe we'll hear much out of Slade until spring. Then he'll start taking your yearlings, but by then we'll be ready for him." He smiled. "We might even find out who's running the show."

Bryson slammed his fist into his open hand. "Whatever you need, son, just ask for it. If I've got it, it's yours." He looked Mason in the eyes. "I don't reckon I have to tell you how glad I am to have you with us. I sure wish you'd let me put you on the payroll."

Mason felt his face flush. He couldn't tell Bryson that Laura had as much to do with his decision as did his contempt for those who tried to get something for nothing. Too, he figured with the rustling, Bryson's money would be getting pretty low. "No, Bryson," he said, "I'll do it my way."

During the next few days Mason pored over the maps Bryson furnished him. He was pleased. Bryson had detailed landmarks and penciled in ravines, odd-shaped trees, canyons, and trails.

Mason knew, though, that to know this country, he'd have to ride it, and look at it from every angle. Things never looked the same from all sides. He'd see the country in his own way, in his own time.

On the sixth day a wind, helped by the slope of the mountains, started a warming trend. A thaw set in. Winds like this were not uncommon in Montana; up there they called them Chinook winds.

With the warming, Mason was ready to ride. He told Bryson and Laura at breakfast that morning.

"How long you think you'll be gone?" Bryson asked.

Mason shook his head. "No idea. Look for me when you see me."

Laura walked from the stove, where she'd been listening, and briefly placed her hand on his arm. "Be careful, Cole."

He nodded, feeling warmth flood him.

While Mason saddled his black, Curt Tilghman walked up and leaned on the corral gate.

"Cutting out, Mason?"

"Yeah, but I'll be back. Gonna look the country over, get to know it a little." He looked up from tightening the second cinch on his Texas rig. "If you come out of a morning and find a horse missing, I'll have been here. No need to disturb any of you. Just take care of this big black of mine."

"You feel a need for anybody to ride with you Bryson'll probably cut me loose for anything you want."

"Much obliged, Tilghman, but this is something I need more than any of you. You know this country—I don't. I'll give a yell if I need anything."

"Well, you know where to find me." Tilghman ambled back to the bunkhouse.

3

MASON SPENT THE rest of the fall and most of the winter riding the valley. He rode Bryson's ranch as well as all of the others, and knew the Slade layout better than any.

Staying clear of people, Mason saw few riders, and avoided being seen. He believed he knew places, such as box canyons and trails, no one else knew.

Mason rode remnants of trails, made by those who'd been there much earlier than the Indians of the day. Some who listened at Indian camp fires heard them called the old ones. Those ancient peoples had left their mark in many ways.

There were those who had built houses in the undercut sides of mountains. There was sign that some animals who no longer roamed this land had been hunted and slain by a people in a manner not known to the Indian or white man. Mason studied it all, feeling a sense of awe that he was privileged enough to see it.

He rode into and then away from the ranch on several occasions, and stayed overnight a few times to break the loneliness and to stock up on provisions. At times he changed horses in the middle of the night. They knew he'd been there and gone. The men in the bunkhouse visited with him, most times down at the corral while he saddled a fresh horse. It was these nocturnal visits that caused Laura keen disappointment.

The morning dawned with a cloudless sky and enough chill in the air to warrant a coat. Laura turned from the corral fence, knowing Cole had changed horses. This walk to the corral had become a morning ritual with her.

She admitted to herself that the tall, quiet man from Texas had come to mean a lot to her. She berated herself. Cole never paid her special attention. Why, when he stayed overnight, he talked to her father almost exclusively. And other nights he talked to no one.

"Cole's been here," she announced when she entered the kitchen.

Her father looked up from the papers spread out on the table, a tenderness showing in his face that she knew he reserved only for her.

"You like that young man a great deal, don't you, honey?"

"Oh Pa, I really do," she admitted with a sigh. "He's never paid much attention to me, but I've never met a man like him." She'd always laid it on the line with her father, and she wasn't going to change now.

"Yes, honey, Mason is different. Not very often in a lifetime are we fortunate enough to meet a man like him." Bryson pulled her into his arms.

"Mason's honest and straightforward," Bryson continued. He's a strong man—the kind who'll help change this land for the best.

"He may be the fastest man living with those guns of his, but doesn't depend on them. From all I've heard, he only uses them when forced to."

Bryson held her from him a moment and looked into her eyes. "He'll be one of the few who'll be able to lay his guns aside once we have law in this land of ours. But for now thank God we have men like him, or we'd be forever knuckling under to renegades like the Slades." He folded her close to him again.

Laura liked the comforting feeling of safety and security she had when her father held her like this.

"Honey, I like Mason, but I wish you didn't care for him so much. With the days ahead of us—rough days—something could happen to him, or, when it's over, he may just saddle up and head for Texas."

Laura said, "Oh no he won't. I'll rope and hogtie him before I let that happen. At least he's going to know how I feel before I let him just ride out."

Bryson threw back his head and roared. She liked to hear him laugh like this; lately, he'd not had much cause to do so.

"A young lady don't just up and tell a man she's set her cap for him."

"This young lady will, Pa. That's how you raised me, and I'm not changing now." Laura looked toward the window, her mood shifting. "I wonder where he is and if he's all right."

Mason was just fine. He was hunkered down by a fire, built under a fir with low-hanging branches, so as to disperse the smoke as it lifted through them.

He'd used this site several times. It was far up the side of the mountain overlooking the Slade place. From here he studied the comings and goings of anyone belonging to that outfit.

He had a pretty good estimate of the number of hands operating out of there—fifty, give or take a few—and knew where their herd was bunched, when they changed the watch, and how many men were on each watch.

He figured there were about fifteen cowhands down there, which left about thirty-five gunhands—a small army, and rough odds for the honest ranchers to buck.

He pushed back his hat and impatiently raked his fingers through his thick black hair. At West Point, he'd studied tactics and strategy and then had applied what he'd learned while engaged in combat during the War Between the States. Now, he was trying to apply the things he'd learned once again, to plot the manner in which they should fight the Slades, with their far superior numbers.

We don't have to fight this thing like war, he thought. Use a hit-and-run operation. Hit them where it hurts and run like hell. Got to be sure to always have a way out. Don't want to be caught and have to fight the way the Slades dictate.

Mason was satisfied that he had it figured right. He threw the rest of his coffee on the fire and covered the embers with dirt. Certain the fire was out, he mounted. Not having been in town for several weeks, he thought it a good idea to see what was happening.

Later, a glance at the sun showed that the ride to town had taken about four hours. Careful to draw little attention to himself, Mason approached from the back of the livery and was stabling his horse when he heard Murtry come from his living quarters.

"Thought you'd left these parts," Murtry said. Then with a twinkle in his eyes he continued, "If Miss Laura wasn't so dadblamed pretty I reckon you might have. When I thought on the matter a little, I knew I'd be seeing you."

Mason said, "If I hadn't owed you a livery bill, reckon I just might have left. But seeing as how you might go broke without my frequent business, I decided to stick around awhile."

Murtry said, "I'm sure glad you did, Mason. Bryson, Laura, me. . . ." He spread his hands. "Hell, the whole town needs you. Where you been?"

"Riding, Murtry, riding all over this straight-up-and-down country." Mason sighed.

"What you doin' in town?" Murtry slipped his pipe out of his shirt pocket and tamped rough-cut into it. Then, without lighting it, he said, "The Slades made a lot of noise, figured to nail yore hide to the wall. When you didn't show up in town for so long, they figured they'd scared you off. Far as I know, ain't none of 'em in town right now."

Mason said, "Last I saw any of them they didn't have a name for me. Reckon they do now?"

Murtry shook his head. "They've called you a lot of things, but Cole ain't been one of 'em." He rubbed the beard stubble on his jaw. "Why'd you go only by the name of Cole all this time? How you figger ain't nobody really knows what you look like?"

"I've given that a pretty good bit of thought, Murtry." Mason pulled a straw from a hay bale and stuck it in his mouth. "The only thing I can figure, when I've had a gunfight, people watch my hands—not my face. After I fire, they're lookin' at the other man to see him fall. By the time they look back to me, I'm gone. And I've used my first name to keep anyone from tying me to my father's ranch."

Murtry struck a lucifer on his boot sole and put the light to his pipe. "You know, with your reputation, I still ain't never heard nobody describe you, even close. I've heard tell you were tall, short, skinny, fat, ugly, mean, plus a lot of good things—you name it.

"But, ain't never heard tell you was tall, broad shouldered, and not a bad lookin' gent to boot. Naw, they ain't never drawed you like that.

"With that in mind, I just kept what I know of you to myself. Far as I can figger, no one's tied you in as being *Cole*, the gunfighter." He puffed thoughtfully, then blew out a great cloud of smoke.

"Yore daddy know about your rep?"

Mason shook his head. "Far as I ever figured it, he only knows he taught me how to use a gun and when to use it. He had some of the best fighting men anywhere riding for him, and they taught me all they knew about weapons—fast draw, knuckle and skull fighting, how to use a Bowie and throwing knife.

"Pa hired fighting men because his ranch is right in the middle of Lipan, Kiowa, and Comanche country. We've always had war on our hands down there." He looked toward Murtry's quarters. "I hate to ask, being it's nothing but cow dip, but you got any a that stuff made you call coffee?"

After listening to Murtry's defense of his coffee, Mason went on. "I've been away from home a lot. There was the war, and since then I've ramrodded trail herds to the north country, ridden for other brands, trapped, even lived with the Sioux for a couple of years.

"This time, though, I took a herd to Montana for Pa, and he said for me to come back by way of Santa Fe—see if I could find some good graze out this way. If I find any, I'll buy it. Have to stop by the bank, set up a transfer of money—" He stopped in midsentence. Murtry was shaking his head.

"Be careful there. This new banker we got here *may* be all right, but he's smooth, too smooth. Don't tip your hand. Meet 'im and make up your own mind." Murtry shrugged. "He may be all right, but somethin' about him just don't set right with me."

Mason had been sitting on a bale of hay. He stood and brushed off his breeches. "Thanks for the tip. I'll play my cards close."

He twisted his gunbelt and settled it comfortably on his hips. "Think I'll get a drink and some dinner. Be a good idea for you and me to stay clear of each other where people will see us until we find out which way the wind is blowing."

He walked down the street, looking carefully at horses and their brands. There were two horses tied in front of the general store, and a buckboard a little farther down the street. The horses were branded with a Lazy S; the buckboard team were each branded with a Box D. Nothing to worry about there.

The saloon had one hip-shot horse tied to the front rail, but the Slade Box S was not in evidence, so Mason went in. A glance showed he had the place to himself except for a young puncher sitting at the far end of the bar.

A slight lift of eyebrows was the only indication the bartender was surprised to see him.

Mason walked over and stood against the wall where the bar curved into it. He asked for a beer.

When the bartender placed it in front of him, Mason took a long swallow and set it back on the highly polished surface. The beer tasted good, for even though it was early spring, the day had settled in hot and still, and the brew was ice cold.

Mason said to the bartender, "This is the coldest beer I've tasted since leaving Montana. I like it best this time of year."

The bartender leaned across the bar. "My name's Barkley, they call me Red," he said, holding out his hand. Then so low the cowhand sitting at the far end could not hear, he continued, "I seen you a couple times before, Dodge City, and San Antone. I don't like what's happening to this town.

"Glad to see *you* decided to stay around. I've said nothing about who you are, and won't." He shrugged and sort of grimaced. "Anyway—count me as a friend when the time comes you need one—and believe me, that time's a-comin'."

Mason was beginning to feel at home in this town. He'd never felt this way before, not even on his father's Big Bend ranch.

He gripped Barkley's hand. "Thanks. Friends are what will count pretty soon." He drained his glass and stepped away from the bar.

"Think I'll make the acquaintance of the banker. Like to know where he stands."

Barkley made a swipe at the bar with a dirty rag. "Form your own opinion—and don't judge the book by its cover."

"That's the second time I've been given that advice." Mason walked over and shouldered through the bat-wing doors.

At the edge of the boardwalk he glanced at the sun and judged it to be about two-thirty, still time to see the banker before closing. Stepping into the dusty street, Mason angled toward the bank.

Wherever men talked of him, the only name used was Cole. No one had ever heard his last name as far as he knew, and he decided to use it in talking to the banker.

"President in?" he asked the teller when he had walked into the cool semi-darkness of the bank.

The mousey little man seemed to be overly impressed with his position. Mason had met others like him.

"Do you have an appointment?"

"No, but I'm telling you I am going to see him. Now, point out his office to me."

Mason squelched the harsh edge of his anger. He was tired and hungry and a little ashamed of taking it out on this little man, but not ashamed enough that he didn't intend to have his way. He didn't like getting the runaround.

Mason glanced about the room and saw a door on the right-hand side behind the counter. He headed for it, the teller following, telling him he couldn't just barge into Mr. Hamilton's office.

Mason reached the door and, casting the teller a cold, contemptuous glance, opened it.

The man behind the desk was not what Mason expected. He stood, and Mason saw he was every bit as tall as himself, but heavier by twenty or thirty pounds. Soft, Mason judged, too much easy living, but a cool customer. The intrusion didn't seem to shake him.

Hamilton walked around the desk, smiling, his hand extended. Mason noted that the smile was tight, forced, and despite the curve Hamilton put to his lips, his eyes remained cold.

"May I be of assistance?" he asked. "I'm Neal Hamilton."

Mason grasped his hand. "Mason's the name, and yes, I believe you may."

"Well, sit down and let's see what the problem is."

Mason allowed himself a slight smile at Hamilton's assumption he had a problem.

He took the chair, thinking to see Hamilton's reaction to someone else coming into the valley with the notion of buying land.

If he had it figured right, Hamilton was lending money to ranchers, with their land as collateral. And, with the Slades stealing their beef, when their notes came due they couldn't market enough cattle to cover the amount owed.

Foreclosure gave Hamilton land worth many times what the loan had been. Mason had nothing on which to base his suspicions, but he thought there was a good chance Hamilton and Slade were in cahoots.

Pointing to an open humidor, Hamilton offered Mason a cigar, which he accepted.

"I'm looking for land, good grass, with water. I don't need cattle. I'll bring them from Texas. Thought you might be carrying the mortgages on several of the ranches around here, or know of those who want to sell their spreads."

Hamilton sat a little straighter.

"No." Hamilton's voice came out soft, silky. "The ranchers around here are in pretty good shape, very little indebtedness. I don't know of any who are thinking of leaving. There really isn't room for another ranch of any size in this valley. You might look down around Santa Fe. There's pretty good grass down there."

Mason had gotten what he came for. Hamilton lied with every word. The ranchers were not in good shape. Mason had found most of them owed the bank money, a goodly bit of money, but not so much they couldn't pay off their loans *if* they had a normal roundup.

The way things were going, the ranchers would not have enough cattle left to make the fall gather worthwhile, and they worried about making the payments when the notes came due.

As for Santa Fe, most of that was old Spanish land grants owned by direct descendants of the original Spanish dons. They'd not part with their land for any price.

"I'll stay here." Mason's words were hard, the quality of them indicating he'd consider no other area. "Something might open up. If it does I'll take advantage of the opportunity."

Hamilton's face reddened, but he controlled his emotions.

"Well, sorry I couldn't help you. You're making a mistake by staying here. People will not take kindly to it if you try to horn in, try to take advantage of any misfortune," Hamilton said. His words contained a thinly veiled threat.

"Well now, maybe they take more kindly to your scheme. You're such an upstanding citizen it would hardly be proper for poor uneducated ranchers to question *your* motives." Mason's harsh words fell between them, as unmistakable as a thrown gauntlet.

Mason saw Hamilton understood perfectly. There was a new player in the game.

Now he'd wait for Hamilton's response. He didn't expect words; they'd been said. The next response would come in the form of action. He spun on his heel, walked out, and headed for the saloon.

This time, other than the bartender, Mason was the only one in the place. Barkley drew a beer and slid it down the bar to him. Mason caught it and drank deeply.

"Well," Barkley asked, "what do you think of Hamilton?"

"I think he'll make one hell of an enemy, and I let him know I'm on to his game, that he could count on me as nothing but an enemy." Mason showed Barkley a grim look. "He thinks I'm out to take over the valley, not that I intend to help the ranchers."

Barkley nodded, his face serious. "Now all you have to worry about is the Slade bunch *and* Hamilton. And by my reckoning they may be one and the same."

Mason said, "Odd you should say that. I've been thinking along the same lines. Would you keep your eyes and ears open, see if there might be a tie-in between the two? I may be wrong—hope I am—but Hamilton comes off too slick." He shook his head. "Maybe most bankers are that way. Never been associated with many of them, so I wouldn't be a good judge.

"I'm gonna get back out to Bryson's place and see what's going on out there. I'll drift in and out of town. Before I cut out, though, think I'll stop in the stores, try to get sense of how the townspeople feel."

Barkley said, "Yeah, do that, but to my way of thinking, they're as tired of Slade as we are. Don't figger they got much opinion about Hamilton yet. He don't seem to be in the market for town businesses so they may not be too quick to line up with the ranchers."

"That being the case, they may think Hamilton's a right fine citizen."

"Don't judge 'em wrong, Mason. They think pretty high of the ranchers and their families. I'd be surprised if you don't git the same feeling about them I got."

Mason left and drifted from store to store, bought a few odds and ends, gabbed awhile in each, being careful to stay clear of direct questions, but still evaluating the people he met. Used to trusting first impressions, he believed Barkley to be right. They seemed for the most part like a solid, respectable bunch.

When he picked up his horse, he filled Murtry in on what had happened. Murtry said, "Young'un, I reckon I done made yoreself the most pizen mean enemy you might've ever throwed yore rope over. Reckon you could've looked all over the territory and not found a meaner one."

"Why do you say that?" Mason asked.

"Well, I ain't told this to nobody—don't reckon I will till I know more'n I do now—but I spent some time down Lincoln County way after I worked for yore pa. I seen Hamilton down yonder and I didn't like him then any more'n I do now."

"Figure you might be right, Murtry, but we'll have to have a lot more to go on than we have now. He's smooth, real smooth, but lets his feelings show around his eyes. That little fault'll get 'im a gut full of lead someday."

He mounted, lifted his hand in a careless wave, and rode out. Murtry's "Be careful, boy" followed him out the door.

4

MASON RODE WARILY, staying off the beaten trails, careful not to be skylined. It was for this reason he didn't blunder into the middle of six Box-S riders, with Bart Slade at their head.

Seeing them, Mason glanced at the swell of ground hiding him from view. He hoped he could remain hidden until they passed, but after studying the situation a moment, he knew it was hopeless; the swell just wasn't high enough.

The odds were bad, but surprise might tilt them in his favor. If he couldn't ride around trouble, he'd always found it best just to ram into it head-on.

He drew both guns and rode out where the riders could see him. They started to reach, hesitated, and grabbed the apple, hands in plain sight, obviously seeing Mason had his full of .44's.

"I thought you'd smartened up and left these parts," Slade said.

"Figured to stick around and see what kind of game you were playing." Mason glanced at the men behind Slade. "Just keep your hands full of pommel."

"Are you calling me a crook?" Slade asked.

Mason lifted an eyebrow. "That's what I'm doing." He waved his right-hand gun. "And I don't think you're dumb enough to draw against a stacked deck."

Slade's riders had started to bunch up, obviously in hopes of hiding their hands so one of them could get a gun into play.

"Bunch up anymore, I'll thin you out. See you better that way," Mason said. "Now spread again, just a little." He thumbed the hammer back on both Colts. "*Now!*"

Their mamas hadn't raised any stupid children. The way they quickly reined horses apart was almost as if they'd seen a rattler in their midst. Mason allowed himself a small smile. "Now, very careful-like, unbuckle your gunbelts."

He watched the belts drop. "All right, now your saddle guns, shuck 'em, throw them in that pile," he said, indicating the loose pile of hand guns. When the last one dropped, he nodded. "Now move out."

Still loosely bunched, they reined their horses around. This was the time Mason figured one of them might take a chance—and he was right.

He saw the flicker movement of a hand and fired. The rider, knocked backward in his saddle, straightened and grabbed frantically for the pommel, then with a surprised expression looked at his chest. There was a small, round, black hole there beginning to seep a red stain onto his shirt. The rider slid slowly from his saddle. He was dead when he hit the ground, his hand still clutching the snub-nosed hideout he'd had concealed in his shirt. Not a horse had moved; like most western horses, they were gun-broke.

Mason motioned to Slade. "Pick him up and get out of here."

When Slade had the dead rider tied across his saddle, he said, "You're good with those guns, but not good enough to last around here. You been lucky so far, but my time is coming. You can bet on it."

The acrid smell of powder smoke hung heavily in the still air. One shot and the smell was there. Mason punched out the spent shell and shoved another into the loading gate.

He watched the riders disappear over the brow of the hill and thought how right Slade was. He *had* been lucky, very lucky. He would have to be even more careful now. Every time he had a run-in with the Slade bunch, a different group of riders saw him, and would, the next time, know him.

It was getting dark. In this mountain country when the sun dropped behind the mountains, night set in, even though the peaks were still bathed in light.

Riding relaxed, Mason thought he caught a faint fragrance on the high mountain air, mixed with pine and spruce. He continued down the trail as long as his tracks could be seen. They would think he'd stayed on the trail, and by sun-up he'd have had a good night's sleep and be long gone.

When it darkened, he kneed the black at a right angle to the trail and headed toward the higher slopes.

Mason spent that night high up the side of the valley. He built no fire, for even a small blaze could be seen from a distance. He ate a cold biscuit, rolled up in his blanket, and went to sleep.

It was still dark when he awoke. He tied his bedroll behind his saddle and wished for a fire. A cup of hot coffee would warm him and taste good too. He tried to flex the stiffness from his muscles, but it didn't work too well.

He reached for his gunbelt, swung it around his waist, and buckled it. He tied holsters to his thighs and checked his guns. Only then did he swing into the saddle, thinking it must be about twelve miles to the Circle B. He wanted to talk to Bryson, and, he admitted to himself, he wanted to see Laura again.

Through narrowed eyes, he gazed into the distance, and gauged that he'd reach the Circle B about noon, if he didn't run into trouble.

Riding, Mason saw that every bunch of cows had several healthy young calves frisking around the edges. If Slade would leave the ranchers alone, he thought, they would have very little trouble paying off their debts. His thoughts drifted back to Laura.

When he first rode into this valley, all he'd had on his mind was a warm meal, a drink, a bed, checking for available land, and then heading for Texas.

His father's ranch would be his and his brother Clay's one day, but he wanted to look at a spread and know it was there because he'd built it. Only in that way would it be a part of him.

Until now he had done the things that any top hand would do for the brand, but he had built nothing for himself. The things he called his own were those he'd bought and paid for—his horse, his saddle, and his guns. Very little to measure a life by.

The lonely camps, endless trails, drifting from a reputation he didn't want, yet adding to it in the next town or lonely coulee surrounded by Indians, always fighting, never putting roots down—he wanted to put all of that behind him.

A woman, a home, and eventually children had been in his thoughts more and more. He'd never been able to put a face to the woman he envisioned spending his life with—until now. That slip of a girl, Laura; her was the one he now saw when he dreamed.

Mason rode into the ranch yard just as Cook was striking the dinner bell. He put his horse in the barn, gave him grain, forked some hay, and, after giving him a quick rubdown, went to the pump and washed up. Then, feeling better, he headed toward the cookshack, walked in, and sat down as though he were there for every meal.

Curt Tilghman glanced at the rider next to him and said through a mouthful of beans, "You notice a stranger around here lately? Saw somebody out at the barn a while ago, an' now seems like there's one more chair filled here at the table."

Mason looked down at his plate, then cast a sour look at the circle of grinning cowboys around the table. "Tilghman, I was so hungry when I wandered in here that all I could think of was surrounding a whole pile of this chow before saying howdy. Consider it said." He stuck his fork into a chunk of steak and mumbled, "Reckon it's all right to eat now?"

"That there's a hungry man if I ever seen one," Tilghman said. "Let's leave him alone and let him fill up, then maybe he'll give us a minute of his time before he goes up to see the Boss. If that's who he's goin' up there to see."

Mason felt the blood rush to his face. Damn, here he was, blushing like a green-tailed schoolboy, he thought, but it warmed his insides to know these men thought enough of him to josh him around.

After putting away enough to feed a haying crew and drinking three cups of coffee that could float a horseshoe, he pushed back from the table.

"Boy, if you eat like that all the time, we'll have to raise Cook's pay, or put on extra help when we know you're coming," Tilghman said.

Ignoring the crack, Mason said, "I'm going up to see Bryson. Like for you to be there. Need to talk about some things and don't want to say them twice."

"Be along in a minute. Got a couple of jobs I want to get the crew started on first."

Mason stopped by the bunkhouse to shave. He put on a clean

shirt and headed for the main ranch house.

In answer to his knock, Bryson yelled, "Door's open, come on in. Come back to the kitchen. Tilghman and Laura are back here."

The odors from the kitchen lured Mason back despite his having just finished a big meal. Laura put a steaming cup of coffee in front of him and turned to pick up a slice of apple pie, still hot from the oven.

"Don't reckon Mason's got room fer any pie, Miss Laura. He just ate 'bout half a steer over in the grub shack, so you might as well save that pie fer one a the crew who'll appreciate it more."

"Laura, don't pay any attention to that broke-down, stove-up, wore-out old puncher there. He's just jealous 'cause his stomach isn't in shape to handle food since he got so old."

Laura placed the pie in front of Mason, shaking her head but obviously pleased that he and Tilghman got along so well.

After a couple of bites Mason looked at her. "If you can cook like this, think I'll take you back to Texas—give you a steady job just cooking for me."

"Careful, cowboy, I might hold you to that," Laura said, also with a kidding tone, but somehow when he looked into her eyes, he knew neither of them were joking.

In the embarrassed silence that followed, Bryson cleared his throat and said, "Tilghman tells me you have something to say. Well, let's get started."

Mason filled them in on all that had happened, including his meeting with Hamilton at the bank and his run-in with the Slade bunch on the trail.

He said, "I may be wrong, but if Slade and Hamilton aren't working together, the games they're playing will still help each other and hurt you ranchers whether that's their intent or not."

Laura, Bryson, and Tilghman each nodded. Laura put their thoughts into words. "I agree with what you're saying, but what can we do about it? We don't have any gunhands."

Mason said to Bryson. "Are there many of the ranchers, big or small, that owe Hamilton money?"

"Yeah, I'd say most do," Bryson said. "Probably not one of us owes a great deal, but all of us have backed our loans with land. Hamilton wouldn't let us use cattle as collateral."

Mason leaned back in his chair. "That's about the way I had it figured. Slade rustles the cattle and when time comes to pay up there aren't enough yearlings or full-grown cattle to sell. Slade gets the money from the rustled cattle, Hamilton forecloses on the ranches, and ends up with all the range around here."

"Well, the fat's in the fire if it's like you think," Bryson said. "But what can we do about it?"

"I figure to turn rustler." Mason's words dropped in the middle of them like a cow patty.

"Wait a minute, boy, what are you saying?" Bryson was clearly shocked.

"What's fair for the goose is fair for the gander. If they steal our cattle, we'll steal them back, and along with that, anything else that'll help to put them out of business, permanently, including not being particular whether they're our cows or his. This is war, Bryson, and I think we can beat them at their own game."

"How you plan to do this?"

"I'll need men—good men. I'm counting on you and the other ranchers to get them. Reckon the next move is to get the ranchers together for a meeting. Think you can handle that part of it, Bryson?"

"You bet I can," Bryson said, then frowned. "But I can't say how many will go along with it. For that matter, there are some who'll not be willing to fight."

Mason felt his face harden. "If they're not willing to fight for what's theirs, then they're not the kind of people it's going to take to make the West a safe place to live and raise families. If they don't fold with this situation, then it'll be some other thing that'll run them out."

Mason waited for what he'd said to sink in, then added, "As hard as it may sound, they're not the kind of people you'll want for neighbors. You'll need better than them to settle this country."

Mason had seen their kind during the War Between the States. They hired mercenaries to do their fighting for them. As always, that type of people thought dead was the worst thing that could happen; honor and freedom meant nothing when their hides were in danger.

Mason said, "I don't want anyone other than us to know how

I plan to fight Slade. The other ranchers only need to know that we need men—nothing else."

He added, "I'll tell my plan to the men I choose to ride with me. If any of them want to back out, then of course that will be their privilege." He raised an eyebrow. "Oh, I know it's a gamble, but a calculated one. I don't believe any man I choose will take the easy way out."

"Count me in." Tilghman stuck out his hand. "I'll ride with you."

"Me too," Laura chipped in.

Mason tried to stifle a smile, then shook his head. "No. Everything's going to have to look natural around here, just as it is on the other spreads. We'll be riding hard, sleeping wherever we happen to be at nightfall. We'll get fresh mounts at night. Much as I'd like to have you both along, you'll be needed here. And you," Mason said to Laura, "little wildcat, do you really think your father would let you go—or that I would?"

Before Laura could respond, Bryson said, "You can bet your prize saddle I wouldn't."

A glance at Laura showed her blush and look down at the table.

Mason looked at each of them in turn. They all gave him a slight nod of approval.

"All right then. If you can set up a meeting for three days from now, I'll be back. There are a couple of things I need to do in the meanwhile." He turned to go out the back door.

Laura headed him off. "If you're going so soon I'll walk down to the barn with you."

They walked in silence, a comfortable quiet that cloaked them. Mason knew there would be rough times ahead, and times like this would be few. He would have liked to stay awhile and enjoy it before the fracas started, but it was time to get moving.

He felt Laura's eyes on him as he threw the saddle blanket across his horse's back. The contact was so strong as to feel almost physical. He glanced at her over his shoulder and caught a look of both fear and something else—a softness, a caring look that he was afraid to interpret. He turned square to her and held out his hand. She came to him and took his hand in her two small ones.

"What's the matter, little one? You look as though you're afraid of something. Don't be fearful of me. . . ."

"Oh, never *of* you, Cole—*for* you," she broke in. "Every time you ride out, I don't know if I'll ever see you again."

"Whoa now," Mason said, "I'll always come back." He pulled her against him and she laid her head on his chest.

"It's . . . it's just that so much is happening now. This used to be such a quiet, peaceful valley. Now everybody seems afraid. They even seem fearful of standing on their own two feet and fighting for what is rightfully theirs, and . . . and I'm worried that they'll stand back and let you do it for them. It's just not fair!"

Mason cupped her chin in his hand, tilting her head so he could look directly into her eyes.

"Does it really mean that much to you?" he whispered, afraid of the answer but having to know. It was what he read in her eyes that gave him his answer, far more than what she said.

Her eyes never wavered. "Yes, Cole, it really means that much to me." She pushed away from him. "Now you go do whatever it is you must do. I'll be here."

He looked into her eyes a long moment, memorizing the soft contours of her face, then brushed her cheek with the backs of his fingers and turned to finish saddling.

Before riding from the ranch yard, Mason twisted in the saddle to see Laura still standing in the barn doorway. He waved; she waved back.

He rode slowly, wondering how Laura had said so much, yet used so few words. He pondered whether Bryson knew of her feelings for him, and whether he would approve, especially since Mason had a reputation as a gunfighter. Not just a gunfighter. Along with that, he was also considered to be one of the most dangerous men alive. It was a reputation he was not proud of. But these were times, he knew, when a man had to be good with guns, because there was little law in these parts.

Most in the West were solid law-abiding citizens, but there were others—vicious, unscrupulous men who held in contempt those who stayed within the law. They held the view that if a man could not defend his property, then it belonged to those who were strong enough to take it, and only a fast gun could keep them from it. Guns were the tools of their trade.

While riding, Mason swept the terrain with his gaze. There were many who wanted him dead, but would not face him in a stand-up gunfight; an ambush was more their style. So he watched, staying below the crest of hills and not moving into a clear area until he was sure he was the only one who would be there.

He stepped from his saddle and slipped to the top of one of these hills to peer over. This time he wasn't the only one in the area. Two punchers were hazing a small bunch of cows toward Slade's Box S.

Mason again checked each ravine and swell of land to be sure that the two he was looking upon were the only ones. He saw no others.

The route they took would bring them within a hundred yards of where he crouched. He waited.

When they were close enough for him to be heard, he called, "Hold it right there. I'm holding a .44–.40 on you, and I don't miss from a hell of a lot farther than this."

He watched as they halted their horses, obviously confused as to his exact whereabouts. Not willing to take a chance, they faced his voice.

"What you want with us?" one asked.

"Just ride, easy-like, toward me. I'll tell you when to stop." They did as they were told. When they were some twenty yards off, Mason said, "That's far enough."

Mason stood, his rifle slung across his back. He was holding a .44 in each hand. "Now, on this side of your horses so I can see you, step down. I want to talk a bit."

They did as he said. He walked to them, and drawing closer, he recognized them. They'd been with Bart Slade on the trail that day.

Mason shook his head. "What do you think I should do with you? Here you are, driving cattle that don't belong to you toward the Box S. Most folks would think you're stealing them." He frowned, shook his head, then pushed his hat back from his brow. "Me, I reckon I'd just have to figure it like most others, and thinking that, I'd figure to hang you from the closest tree."

Mason holstered his left-hand gun and untied the pigging string holding his rope on his saddle. "I suppose maybe I'd best see if I can find a good sturdy tree. Hate like hell to use a new rope on you, though." A glance showed they had turned a pasty color.

"Aw, now you ain't gonna hang us, are you?" Those last words came out in a squeak.

Mason didn't indend to, but he thought if he could scare them bad enough, he might convince them to leave the country.

The rustler had hardly finished speaking when Mason saw his eyes shift to the side, a snake-like glint in them. Mason twisted and dropped. A fiery streak creased his shoulders, followed by the sharp report of a rifle, off to the east.

He hit the ground, rolled, and fired at the two rustlers. They were drawing their hand guns, but neither of them cleared leather before Mason's slugs caught them dead-center in their chest.

He rolled again, not waiting to see if the rustlers fell, and shifted his .44 to bear on where the shot had come from. Dirt from another shot kicked into his face. He saw his attacker levering another shell into the chamber of his rifle. Mason fired both .44s at once and saw the man's head explode. Mason counted that as a miss; he'd figured to hit the man in the chest.

Mason rolled again, to face the first two. There was no need—they were lying where they'd started their draw, a thin cloud of powder smoke drifting across them—a fitting marker for their end.

Holstering his left-hand gun, Mason approached them cautiously. He kicked their weapons out of reach. He'd seen men take several slugs in the body and still have fight left, too dumb to know they were dying.

He found the horse of the one who'd tried to ambush him and led it to the rustlers' horses. It took but a short while to throw his attackers across the saddles and tie their hands to their feet under the horses' bellies. A whack across the rump sent them toward the Box S.

Mason mounted and headed back toward Bryson's place, but only to confuse any who might try to track him. He knew that the shots might have been heard.

After about a mile he dipped down into a small stream, walked his horse in it a few hundred feet, then headed straight toward the escarpment. If they wanted to follow him, they'd not take him by surprise. He rode into every aspen thicket, and before he left, he carefully searched for sign of pursuit. By mid-afternoon he felt certain that no one followed.

5

MASON THOUGHT HE had found where the Slades held the rustled cattle between drives, but he was not sure. Wanting a closer look at the hidden basin, he rode cautiously toward it, but planned to avoid a fight if he could.

While scouting the valley during the winter, he'd found the basin, and even though he was looking for places that were not obvious, he'd almost ridden by the opening in the escarpment that gave passage into the great bowl.

The cleft he'd found extended about two hundred yards between sheer granite walls. Its floor, covered with fine white sand, told him that water, a great deal of it, had flowed through here in some distant past, and looking at the passage floor, Mason had wondered at the absence of tracks.

He had ridden in only far enough to see that the basin was about ten thousand acres of lush grass with a twenty- or twenty-five-acre lake in the middle. Now he wanted to see all of it, see if there was cow sign—or man sign.

Mason circled wide of all ranch headquarters, and had seen no one since his scrape with the rustlers.

Riding close to the escarpment, he looked up and saw the rimrock from which he had ridden the day he met Laura, and he wondered at the forces of nature that had sheared this land to form the valley, with its wall along one side and mountains on the other three.

It had to have happened long before the coming of man to this wondrous world, before the Ute or Apache, even long before the Ancient Ones he'd heard whispered about during tribal rituals.

He wended his way through a patch of trees and stopped to scan the country before riding into the open. Then, his thoughts turned again to the Ancient Ones.

It was said they knew the secrets of nature. They had passed down some of their knowledge, but much of it had disappeared with them. No one knew when they had left, where they went, or, most puzzling, why they had gone, but they had left more than whispers that they had been here.

There were whole towns built of stone, with wide streets or highways, multistoried dwellings, pottery, and evidence they had raised crops. Mason had seen these things in his journeys, but told no one, for he knew they would tag his report a fantasy.

The Ancient Ones' mastery of irrigation had enabled them to flourish in this arid, hostile environment for several hundred years. They had also devised a sun calendar that precisely depicted when each season began and ended. Mason had been there, walked where they walked and counted himself privileged to have done so. There would be many who would travel this way in the future, he thought, and would marvel that such an ancient civilization had survived in this land.

His gaze swept the walls of the escarpment for sign that the Ancient Ones had traveled this valley. He was looking for chisel marks or paintings on the walls—the type that he had seen west of here—but he saw none.

He rode as close to the wall as its talus base would permit, for it would be easy to miss the fault through which he needed to enter the basin.

Dusk settled on the land, and Mason used more care in searching the sheer granite cliff against which he rode. It would take only a shadow to obscure the opening. Then he saw it, the fold that hid the passage through the escarpment.

Couldn't have timed it better, he thought. He dismounted, took off his boots, and slipped on his moccasins. There was not much chance for a step to make noise on the sandy floor of the opening, but he had to play it safe.

If there was a Slade campsite in the basin, Mason figured to be an unannounced visitor. Reckon I'm just rude that way, he mused. His thought brought forth a smile. There was no one posted outside to guard the entrance, so he closed in on the opening, leading the black.

Noise was inevitable on the talus, but in the passage, it was as though the world had stopped. There were no insect noises, or those of birds; even the sighing of the wind had ceased. Mason shivered at his isolation. He was only a stirring of air as he exited the passage into the basin.

From his vantage point at the inner lip of the passage, he scanned the basin, looking for the wink of a camp fire. He saw none. After the almost total darkness of the passage the sudden light caused him to blink, but he could see well. After his sweeping search, he picked a patch that was darker than the surrounding area, knowing it to be a clump of trees, and headed toward it to set up camp.

Upon reaching the trees, he was pleased. The thicket was mostly aspen, a very old stand, to judge from their size. The older ones had rotted from inside, as they were want to do, and fallen, to provide room for the younger ones to reach for the sun. They were about three hundred yards from the entrance, with some rocky ground in-between.

There was little chance that anyone could slip up on him in the night, but to make his camp even more secure, he gathered brush and twigs and scattered them in a circle around where he'd sleep. The sound of a twig being stepped on would waken him.

Mason didn't make a fire, for he was high on the side of the basin, and it would easily be seen from below—if there were eyes there to see it. He unrolled his bedroll, took a piece of jerky from his supplies, and sat by his saddle. Using his sheath knife, he cut off a bite-sized piece and ate. How many meals had he made of nothing but jerky and water, he wondered, and how many just water.

These were the times Mason liked though—quiet solitude, with only an occasional rustle of underbrush as some night animal scurried about, the hoot of an owl, or the distant, mournful howl of a coyote—and the scent of pines to perfume the air. If the Ancient Ones had been here, something terrible must have happened to drive them away. He slipped under his blanket and, through heavy lids, watched the stars come down to fold him in sleep.

He awoke in chill darkness, still more than an hour until sunup. He rolled over stiffly, sat, and rubbed circulation into his arms. "Damn chill works its way right into a man's insides," he grumbled.

He decided to build a fire, knowing it could be dangerous. He thought he could defend himself here. A glance showed a clear field of fire in front and to the sides, with the granite wall at his back. A man could hold off an army from here. He'd fix a hot meal and coffee; the black would be satisfied with gnawing on that sweet mountain grass yonder.

After a glance at the passage through which he'd come the night before, which revealed no tracks but his own, he prepared breakfast.

The coming of daylight was subtle. It slipped up on a man. The velvety darkness melted into a translucent veil. Mason watched as the sun launched its lances of fire into the basin, from between peaks standing ghostly in the early light.

Below, mist shrouded the valley. He thought of it as a beautiful woman, promising, yet withholding, and as its streamers were nudged by a vagrant breeze, other treasures, known, but unknown, were hinted at.

He cast a lingering glance at the basin below, then looked to see if his coffee was boiling.

By the time he had eaten breakfast and sat spraddle-legged by the fire, sipping his coffee, it was daylight. The deep shadows under the trees and in the ravines were the only hint that night had been here.

From his campsite he had a view of the entire basin. His breath caught in his throat, and for a moment he felt as the Everywhere Spirit must have felt when he looked down upon the virginity of perfect creation.

Mason sighed. He had things to do. He picked up his saddle and walked to his horse.

After saddling the black, he left him ground-reined, and even though he had checked it once, he returned to the mouth of the passage. He had swept out all signs of tracks upon entering the basin the night before. It was as he had left it; the sandy floor was without sign. He returned to the black.

From the mouth of the passage down to the floor of the basin took a couple of hours of close scouting. He crossed and crisscrossed the area, and found no sign of cows, hoofprints, or droppings on the soft topsoil. He was certain now that this basin had never been used by the Slade bunch, or anyone, for longer, hundreds of years longer, than he had been in this world.

Mason had come here looking for a place in which rustled cattle had been held, and he had found an unspoiled, virgin land. He wondered if anyone had ever been here.

Now he felt the basin could be looked upon without danger. At times the grass was high enough to brush the bottoms of his stirrups. Looking at it, Mason marveled that one acre could feed as many cattle as ten, maybe even twenty, acres of West Texas graze. He looked from grass, to stream, to patches of tall aspen, and found himself thinking of it as his.

It was then he saw, chiseled into the granite wall, the forms of many hunters, arms raised, apparently waving to scare their quarry. An animal—it looked to be a shaggy-haired mammoth, gone from the vastness of this continent long ago—was racing toward what looked to be meant for a cliff. Mason rode closer to the wall. At the base of the cliff a pile of mammoths had been chiseled into the surface.

It had taken a great deal of patience, and not a little talent, to carve these things into the solid stone. It appeared that the hunters had wings, or perhaps they were meant to be robes, and the absence of weapons showed that these petroglyphs predated known history.

There had been people here, even before the Ancient Ones. Mason found two other carvings. Each depicted a hunter in some attitude of attack. He studied them and rode on, wondering that there had been such a lapse of time between man's visits to this Eden.

Now, Mason was certain he was the first to come here in perhaps thousands of years. The animals pictured on the granite surface had been extinct since before the last ice age.

Then, thinking of the entrance, he understood. On the escarpment side of the entrance, there was a fold of granite that closed back on itself. Unless a body rode hard up against the wall, going in the right direction, he could pass within arm's reach and not see the entrance. And the talus close to the escarpment wall prevented riding close.

When Mason had seen as much as time would allow, he decided to ride into town to see Barkley and Murtry. He was curious to learn if they had found out anything.

It was dark when he rode to the livery and stabled the black. He was almost through rubbing him down when Murtry appeared out of the darkness.

The old man sidled up and leaned against the side of the stall. "Hello, boy, see you made it back." He pulled a hay straw from a bale and stuck it in his mouth. Then, as if commenting on the weather, he said, "Seven or eight of the Slade bunch are in town. If you figure to go in the saloon, you'll need someone to watch your back."

Finished rubbing down the black, Mason picked up a pitch-fork and tossed hay into the stall. He said, "I'd just as soon they didn't tie us in as friends—yet. I'll keep my back to the wall anyway." He started to head out, then said, "You see or hear anything?"

"Nope." Then as an afterthought, Murtry added, "Well, yeah, it may not mean much, but . . . well . . . it might too." He poured some grain in the feed box. "Yep, reckon it might."

Murtry frowned. "I seen Bart Slade injun up to the back door at Hamilton's house. He tapped sort of light-like, two times, spaced even, and then slipped in after the lantern inside went dark." He shook his head. "I eased up to the side of the house but couldn't hear nothin'."

Mason said, "Listen, old-timer, don't ever take that sort of chance again. Yeah, it's important, damned important, but I'll take it from here. Besides, I'll need you to get word to Pa later on." Then he asked, "Is there a telegraph in this town?"

"Yep, just finished puttin' it in 'bout two months ago. The operator is four square. We can trust him." Murtry scratched the back of his head. "Don't hardly seem likely we got us a telegraph but no law to speak of. Last marshal got his self killed 'bout a week 'fore you come into the valley. Some said a horse throwed 'im."

"We might need the telegraph later on." Mason twisted his holsters into place. "Reckon I might as well get on with it. Hope I can avoid trouble."

"Don't bet on it." Murtry's words followed Mason out the door.

When Mason pushed through the saloon's bat-wing doors, all noise stopped as though a blanket had been thrown over the room. He felt the gaze of every man there on him.

A quick glance told him that neither of the Slades was here, but sitting at a table near the bar was a group of Slade riders, two of whom knew Mason. They had been with the bunch he'd had trouble with on the trail.

Keeping his gaze on them, he moved along the wall to the place where the polished surface of the bar connected with it. The space was empty, so he slid into it and placed his shoulders against the wall.

"Beer," he said as Barkley came toward him. The tension was thick. Even the townspeople, who had no chips in this game, seemed to sense that emotions would explode at any second. Barkley slid a mug of beer in front of him.

One of the men from the trail said something out of the corner of his mouth to the rider next to him, then stood. "Looks like an even break this time," he said.

The rider had gunslinger oozing out of every pore, and looking into his eyes, Mason saw no flicker of fear. He knew he was going to have to kill this man, and with that knowledge came the ice, starting at the very core of his being, stifling every emotion.

Regret at having to kill again might come later, but Mason doubted that it would. This was a killer he faced, and he was asking for him to make his play.

"Any man moves a hand, I'll kill 'im," Mason said, so quietly that it was hard to believe they could all hear, but they heard, for every hand stayed in sight.

"All right, gunfighter," Mason said, "my guns are still in leather. You've got your even break. Make the most of it."

Mason looked into the gunman's flat gray eyes. The eyes always gave away what would follow.

Mason drew, knowing as soon as he squeezed off his shot he'd not face this man again. But he wondered at his accuracy, or lack of it, for once again he'd missed hitting where he'd intended. Blood spurted in a steady, strong stream from the gunslinger's throat. Mason had meant to hit him in the center of his chest.

The gunman took a step toward him, his gun angled toward the floor, and then from some deep well of hate he mustered enough strength to squeeze off a shot. It went harmlessly into the rough planks at Mason's feet.

After the rending roar of the shots, the silence was deafening, the acrid smell of gunsmoke suffocating.

Mason holstered his weapon and brought the beer mug to his

lips. There was an explosion of sound. It seemed that everyone talked at once. The Box-S riders started to stand.

"Stay where you are." Mason's voice cut through the noise. "When I finish my beer you can take your garbage out and get him buried—till then stay where I can see you, hands in plain sight."

It was then that he recognized young Bob Brannigan from Bryson's Circle B. He looked at Mason with an awed expression.

He stood and, obviously taking care not to walk between Mason and the Slade men, circled the room to Mason's side.

"I never even seen you draw," he said in a hushed voice. "I guess I seen the best there is at one time or other, but not one of them could shade you."

Mason glanced at him out of the corners of his eyes, careful to keep the Slade riders in view. "Don't ever believe that. There's always someone better—and anxious to prove it." Mason's voice came out flat, tinged with bitterness. He signaled Barkley for two more beers.

When Barkley put the beers on the bar, he said to Mason under his breath, "We've got to talk. See me after I close."

Mason nodded slightly.

He and Brannigan finished their beers. Then Mason said to the Box-S bunch, "Don't move. Leave after me—about five minutes after." He motioned to Brannigan to go ahead of him as he moved along the wall toward the door. Then, with a glance around the room, Mason pushed through the doors and melted into the darkness.

Clear of the doors, he said to Brannigan, "This way." They rounded the corner of the building and ran to the back. "Where's your horse?"

"Tied to the rail in front of the saloon."

"Then you'll have to leave him. Murtry'll get 'im later. Rent another and head out. I need to see someone. I'll be at the ranch tomorrow."

Barkley lived above the saloon, and there was a back staircase to his quarters. Mason took it.

"But—" Brannigan said, and then realized that Mason was no longer with him. "Whew! You're spooky as an Indian."

Mason smiled into the darkness. He could have told Brannigan that you only learned to walk quietly from experiencing fear.

Watching Brannigan head for the livery, Mason climbed the rest of the stairs to Barkley's room. He took only a second to jimmy the lock and enter. His eyes, now used to the darkness, saw that Barkley's quarters were sparsely furnished.

Not lighting a lantern, for fear some curious citizen might come to investigate, he sat in Barkley's one chair and closed his eyes, letting his fatigue take charge. He soon slept.

The door lock rattled. Mason came instantly awake, drew and leveled his .44 at the door, then saw Barkley's silhouette outlined against the light of the hallway.

Barkley struck a match and lit his only lantern before he saw that he was not alone.

"Figured you'd be here," he said.

Without any preliminaries Mason came to the point. "You said you needed to see me." He slipped his .44 back into its holster.

Barkley went to a shelf by the washbasin and took down a bottle and two glasses. He splashed each about half-full and handed one to Mason. He said, "This is far better than what I pass across the bar." Mason nodded his thanks, as Barkley sat on the bed.

Barkley sipped his drink and looked at Mason over the rim of his glass. "Last night, a gunny, headed for the Slade outfit, just in from down Lincoln way, was kind of talkative.

"Said he was surprised to see Hamilton here after making a fortune in the Lincoln County fracas, but that it was no never mind of his. Said he was going out to the Slade place, asked me for directions as to how to get out there."

Barkley set his drink on the floor, took out his makings, and rolled a cigarette. After he had it lit, he said, "Here comes the good stuff. He mentioned as to how thick Bart Slade and Hamilton had been in Lincoln, and that he was surprised they weren't in the ranch together."

Barkley stood and took a couple of nervous turns about the room. "I reckon that pretty well tells us they're running this thing together. Important thing is, Hamilton carries a gun in a shoulder holster. According to that gunny last night he's fast, real fast, faster'n Bart. Knowing this may give you an edge— if you need one.

"When you're around Hamilton, notice he always seems to hold his hands around his lapels like this." He slid his fingers up and down his lapels. "Mason, just think how close those hands are to his shoulder holster."

Mason smiled at Barkley and held out his drink in a toast. Their glasses clinked. "That's about all I ever asked for—an even break. Thanks."

Barkley flushed, obviously pleased but embarrassed by Mason's words. "Well, hell, Mason, if we're gonna whup up on 'em, let's do it right."

Mason tossed off the rest of his drink. "Thanks, Barkley. I better be getting on back to the ranch." He gripped Barkley's hand and added, "This trip was worth the ride."

Barkley said, "You ain't out of town yet. Don't you believe they've give up on finding you. That ranny you killed down in the bar was one of their fastest guns. They want you bad."

Mason agreed. "No, I don't think they'll give up very easy. But, there being only five or six of them, they've spread out all over town. I meet one of them at a time, they're in deep trouble."

"I wouldn't try to stop you." Barkley grinned and reached for the lantern and put it out.

He was talking to an empty room.

Mason crouched under the only window in the barn. It opened out of Murtry's office and sleeping quarters. He tapped softly on the glass. Murtry would be in there this time of night. He got no answer.

They must have put Murtry out of the game, he thought, hoping they'd not hurt the old man. He then pondered the problem of getting into the barn without getting shot.

He figured that one and no more than two guns would be in there against him, and they would both be watching the stable door. Murtry's office would be empty. He knocked a little louder on the window and didn't draw a shot.

He broke out of his crouch and pushed upward on the window. It inched up with a slight scraping sound. Mason eased pressure on it and moved it up a little at a time. It took him about three minutes to open it enough to squeeze through. Slowly, he worked his way across the sill and dropped to the floor underneath without a sound.

He was about to step toward the middle of the room when he sensed his foot against something soft. Crouching, his

exploring hands quickly told him he'd found Murtry, tied
hand and foot.

A hand over Murtry's mouth got him a nod. Mason guessed
the old man wasn't hurt too bad and wouldn't make a sound,
knowing it would bring Slade's riders on the run. Mason
untied him.

Murtry pulled Mason's ear to his mouth. "There's two of
'em," he whispered. "I know one of 'em's in the hay mow.
I could hear him making hisself comfortable up there. I don't
know 'bout the other."

Mason motioned for Murtry to stay put. He stood and,
wraithlike, was absorbed into the dark of the stable.

He moved quietly along the wall, breathing slowly, so as to
make no sound. Where would a man be most likely to stand if
he wanted to surprise someone? He wondered. Most probably
inside the door, to the side. Mason inched toward the door,
stopping every few seconds to listen. It paid off.

He heard the faint, irregular breathing of a man not more
than three feet in front of him. He eased a little closer; then
judging where the man's head would be, he swung his gun.

He felt the man's skull crumple under the blow. Mason
caught him under the arms and carefully lowered him to the
floor.

He knew he'd killed the gunny, but hell, he'd had the same
thought in mind for Mason. Now all he had to think of was the
other one, hiding in the hay mow. The blow to his assailant's
head had made more noise than Mason would have liked. It
was a sure bet it had been heard.

A white man, Mason knew, lacked the patience of the
Indian. An Indian would sit quietly and wait for his enemy
to give away his position by some movement or sound, but
these men Mason stalked were not Indians.

He waited. Finally he heard the almost noiseless scrape of
denim against wood. From the position of the noise, Mason
guessed his ambusher was descending the ladder from the loft.
Mason waited.

It was not long before he sensed, rather than saw, the form
of a man in front of him, slipping toward the door where his
partner had waited.

Mason wanted to do this without having to use his gun.
Shooting would bring the rest of the Slade bunch on the run.

Slipping his .44 into its holster, he pulled his Bowie knife.

While he drew his knife from its scabbard, the gunny stubbed his toe against the body of his partner. He grunted and swore under his breath. Mason dived, swung his knife, and felt it go to the hilt in the man.

He reached for the gunman's mouth, to stifle the inevitable groan when he pulled out his knife. He caught his sagging body in both arms and lowered him to the ground.

Calling over his shoulder, Mason said, "Murtry, bring a light out here."

The glow of the lantern showed that both Slade men were dead.

"Leave them where they are," Mason warned as Murtry reached to drag one of them away. "I'll tie you up again and slip the gag down so's to look like you raked it out of your mouth against the table leg."

He steered Murtry back to the office to set the stage. When he again had Murtry tied, he pulled on the rawhide. "Too tight?"

"Naw, it's fine," Murtry grunted. "You saddle up and get out of here 'fore they find you."

"I'll stick my head back in before I cut out."

His horse saddled, Mason led him to the door of Murtry's office. "When you hear me ride out, start yelling. I'll be long gone before they can get on my trail." He checked Murtry's bindings. "This may not fool 'em, but it'll keep 'em off-balance. They won't be sure we're in this together." Mason mounted and left by the back door.

6

MASON STAYED OFF the trail. Along about daylight he caught a couple of hours' sleep, then moved on. It was pushing midafternoon when he rode into the ranch yard. He threaded his way between and around several buckboards. The hitch rack was full; about twenty horses, he guessed. Looks like a good old country dance, he thought, and headed for the stable.

Before he could open the door, Bob Brannigan appeared at the black's head. "I was beginning to wonder if you'd made it," he said. "I didn't have any trouble last night. Must've been ahead of them all the way." He took the reins from Mason. "I'll take care of your horse. The Boss'll want to see you— an' maybe even Miss Laura."

Mason went to the kitchen door and stuck his head in. Laura and Cook were there. He walked over and pulled out a chair.

Laura didn't say anything, but looked at him, from his head to his feet and back again. Then, she sighed and said, "Glad you got back. You're in time for the meeting." Almost too casually, to Mason's way of thinking, she added, "Everything go all right in town?"

Mason shrugged. "Yeah, pretty quiet. I just scouted around. There were a few things I needed to find out before this meeting. I discovered—"

Before he knew what she was about, Laura was standing in front of him, her little fists pounding him on the chest, her eyes spitting fire.

He grabbed her wrists. "Hey—whoa up here, little one. What've I done to get your dander up?"

"Oh . . . oh, you—" Laura pulled her wrists free and stepped back. "You go into town, get in a gunfight, then don't come home till hours after Bob shows up, and . . . and then you tell me that everything went pretty quiet."

"Reckon Brannigan has been spreading some of Ned Buntline's fiction around."

"Don't you patronize me," Laura sputtered. "One of the ranchers here today saw the whole thing, and it all happened just like Bob said it did. There were seven of Slade's gunmen in that saloon when you sidled in and bucked the whole bunch."

"Well I—" he started then changed the subject. "What are all these people doing here? I thought there would only be the ranch owners."

"Don't think you've sidetracked me, Cole Mason," Laura said. "But, yes, Pa and I talked about it, and I thought if it looked like we were having a fandango it would not create any suspicion on the part of the Slade bunch." She smiled. "And besides, this is a good excuse to have a party. We haven't had one in a long time. After you men have your meeting we'll have a barbecue and some dancin'."

Happy for any excuse to avoid Laura's wrath, Mason said, "Well, if that's the case, I reckon I'd better get me a bath and some clean clothes." Before Laura could answer, he slipped out and headed for the bunkhouse.

Mason felt better. He had gotten rid of the tiredness right along with the trail dust, threw it all out with the bathwater. He was introduced to several ladies as he crossed the yard toward the house. When he entered the large living room, Bryson came over and took his arm.

"We're all here, boy. Let's get you acquainted with everyone." He steered Mason around the room and introduced him to each rancher. There were owners of large and small ranches. Mason could tell almost by looking at them the size of their spread, but there the dissimilarity ended. They all looked worried.

"I'm going to turn this meeting over to Mason. He has a few facts and, I might add, a few well-founded suspicions he wants to share." Bryson was about to sit down and let Mason have the floor when Tom Snelling, one of the ranchers, stood, his hand raised.

"Wait a minute, Bryson. I'd like to get something clear before we get on with the meeting." He looked sort of embarrassed, then squared his shoulders and continued. "All of us here run cattle in this valley."

He looked squarely at Mason. "To my knowledge, Mr. Mason, you have no interests at all, in us, or the valley. I, for one, would like to hear why you are buying into this game, and what you expect to get out of it." Snelling continued looking him square in the eye while he pulled his chair under him and sat down. Several of the ranchers murmured in agreement.

Mason said, "Good question, Snelling. In your shoes, I'd want an answer to that question. First, I'll tell you why I'm here."

Mason told them about driving his father's herd to Montana and, at his father's instructions, swinging back over into New Mexico country to try and spot some good grass for sale.

He told them how he and Laura had met, but downplayed his part in the Apache skirmish, then his meeting with Bryson, and that Bryson had offered him a job, but that he'd declined the offer. He didn't go into why he had decided, finally, to stay on—that is, he didn't tell them that Laura was the reason.

He sat on the corner of the table in the middle of the room, one leg hanging off the edge. "Something made me change my mind," he said. "I found a likely looking spot I'd like to buy, and I don't want to come into an area about to explode into a full-fledged range war. So, I figured to see if maybe I could do something to stop those who are stirring it up. I hasten to add, before you ask, the land I'm interested in does not belong to any of you. My buying it will not, in any way, infringe on your range. That's a promise."

Snelling said, "Sounds like a good enough reason to me." He looked at the rest of the ranchers. "How 'bout you?"

They nodded. Snelling said to Mason, "All right, let's hear the rest of it."

Mason laid it out for them: that Hamilton and Slade had been partners down in the Lincoln county fracas, and his belief that they were still partners and were working their game here. He was honest in telling them he had not one whit of proof, but it made too much sense to ignore.

"Sounds like you have it figured pretty close," Snelling said. "Bryson tells me you have a plan. I think we would all like to hear it and what we can do to help." Once again the others in the room seconded Snelling.

Mason pushed up from the table. "All right, but before I go into the plan I'll tell you this: I sent a telegram to my father and asked him to deposit with Wells Fargo a goodly sum of money for my use. He'll do it because I've never asked anything like this of him before. He'll know it's important."

Mason poured himself a cup of coffee. "The reason I want the money is to cover any mortgage notes you might have with Hamilton, but only if you trust me enough to."

He flicked a glance around the room. "If any of you want no part of this, I can't blame you. There are going to be people hurt. If you want to sell out, I'll give you a fair price for your spread, after I deduct what you owe Hamilton. Those of you who will join in the fight give me your note and I'll pay Hamilton off. I'll carry your mortgage until we can make a drive to the forts."

Mason saw expressions ranging from doubt to acceptance on the faces surrounding him. He swiped his hand through his hair and frowned. "If I were in your saddle, reckon I'd have to wonder why you should trust *me* to hold your mortgage any more than Hamilton.

"Well, let's look at it this way. There must be a lawyer in town you all trust, so, we'll have him draw up papers fair to both of us." A glance indicated he'd won acceptance from most of them. "There's no one going to try to force you to participate in this, and now is the time to say you want no part of it. What do you have to lose?"

Mason paused. "Anybody want out?"

A man he remembered being introduced as Hans Larsen stood. "Me, Mr. Mason. My missus an' me ain't used to this sort of thing. We're farmers, not ranchers. Reckon we'll go back to Ohio. I got twenty-four hundred acres of pretty good land out yonder if you can come over an' make me an offer."

"I understand, Larsen. I'll come over this week," Mason said. He looked around the room. "Anyone else?" No one came forward.

After Larsen left, Mason told them the plan. "I want at least one good man from each of you. I'll pick the men. I'm not going to tell you specifically what we will be doing because the less any of you know, the better for you in case we get tangled up with the law.

"I've told Bryson, vaguely, what we'll do. I believe you all know him well enough to know you can take his word—and trust his judgment.

"I'll ask one last thing of you. Forget we ever had this meeting, and forget all of you, that you ever heard my name.

"I'll be visiting your ranches in the next few days to pick one of your riders to side me." After thanking them, Mason left the room.

He knew there would be reservations on the part of many, and he was counting on Bryson to swing the tide.

Mason visited with Bryson's riders and stepped from one group of ladies to another, getting acquainted, with Laura's help. After giving the men time to lay their cards on the table and hash out their differences, he walked to the corral to look at his horse.

He was edgy, not wanting the plan to fall through. Yes, he thought, there was plenty of land elsewhere—but there wasn't another Laura. He was about to give it up as a lost cause, when the ranchers emerged from the front door.

Bryson's eyes locked with Mason's. He winked and smiled. "Let's eat," was all Bryson said.

Mason exhaled, knowing the plan had been accepted.

The ladies cleaned up after all had eaten their fill. The men collected out at the barn to set hay bales around for seats. While some cleared the center of the floor for dancing, Tilghman sidled softly up to Bryson, who was helping push a wagon to the back of the barn.

"Riders comin' in, Boss. Looks like it might be some of the Slade bunch." Tilghman's words were softly spoken, but Bryson heard them.

"Damn," Bryson said. He seldom cursed, and his reaction only served to deepen the frown on Tilghman's face.

"What you want to do, Boss?"

Bryson looked at Mason. "You think this means trouble?"

"You can bet on it. We better keep the ladies and children in the house until we find out."

Bryson looked at Tilghman. "Go up to the house and make sure the women stay there. Round up the children and get them inside too. Don't alarm 'em. Do it as quietly as possible."

Tilghman left at a trot, and Bryson said to Mason, "Place the men around in spots where we'll have the advantage when we face them."

Most of the men were already in the barn. Mason had no problem in quickly assigning them to places in the hay mow and behind wagons. He sent three into the house. "You, Brannigan, stay here with me."

Bryson bristled. "You're not going out there alone. I'm siding you."

Old Tom Driscoll, one of the ranchers, pulled his rifle out of its scabbard and turned to Mason. "You start the music, son. I'll be right there dancin' by your side." His face broke into a grin. "Whoeee, this might be some kind of fandango after all. Ain't had this much fun since grandma sat in the apple butter."

"All right, men." Mason cut Driscoll short. "Don't start dancing unless I start the music. If it comes to that, cut down every one of them you can get a bead on." His words were little above a whisper, but not so low they couldn't hear.

Bob Brannigan said to no one in particular, "Don't believe any of you ever danced to Mason's tune. He plays music like you ain't never heard before. One second his hand is empty, and the next it's spoutin' lead—and unlike most a them fast-draw artists, *he* hits what he's lookin' at." He looked around. "You'll all know it when Mason opens the dance, 'cause there'll be them what's fallin'."

Mason watched the Slade riders rein their mounts to a stop and dismount at the rack in front of the house. He stepped outside. "We're over here, Slade," he called, recognizing Bart Slade as the lead rider.

Slade spun toward Mason, obviously taken by surprise, expecting to find most of the guests in the house.

"State your business, Slade. Then get out."

Slade's face turned a bright red, but he was no fool. Mason knew that by Slade's reckoning he should be holding high cards in this game and suddenly the tables were turned. Slade was looking at a straight flush, against his two pair, and would lose—not just this hand but his whole poke—if he made a move.

Mason saw the tenseness go out of Slade and knew there would be no gunplay. He didn't want any. The women and children were in too much danger of being hit by a stray bullet or wood splinters, which could tear a person apart just as easily.

"I ask again, Slade. What do you want?" Mason bit out the words. He could see Slade was in full control of his anger, which had turned to a cold, controlled fury.

"Aw, we saw so many people headed this way, we figured you all must be havin' a barn dance." Slade tried a disarming grin, but it was more of a grimace. It did not reach his eyes. "We figured as how we would join in an' have a few dances. It wasn't very neighborly of you folks not to invite us."

"You're not invited. These are decent folks. Now ride on out. That's your invitation. I'll give you another when the time's right. This is not the time."

Slade stood there looking at him, then said, "Can't figure you, cowboy. You don't have a stake here in the valley, yet you seem to have shoved your way into everybody's business.

"I don't even know your name, but there are those who say you have a reputation with those guns. If you do, you had better be real good, when you *do* give me that invitation.

"Now me, being real hospitable, well I might send you an invitation first, but it will be in a time and place of my choosin'."

Without waiting for an answer, Slade grabbed the pommel of his saddle and swung aboard. "Gentlemen," he said, then reined his horse around and kicked him into a gallop, his men close behind.

Mason watched them shrink with distance. He wondered how a man who had apparently been a gentleman in some distant past could have twisted into the sort of man Slade now was. There were many in the West, of good families, who had taken the wrong trail. There were even times in his own past when he could have made the wrong decision.

Mason heard Driscoll, Brannigan, and Bryson exhale at the same time.

"Seems sort of like you was tryin' to push him into a fight, Mason," Driscoll said, his grizzled old jaws working his tobacco up tighter in his jaw.

"Slade wouldn't want a fight once he knew he couldn't call the shots. If we had shown any sign of fear, though, he might have taken a chance. Took a chance and pushed him to the brink." He faced old Driscoll and winked. "It worked, didn't it?"

Driscoll shook his head slowly, then puckered his lips and spit a stream of tobacco juice at a fly sitting on a nearby cow pie. He squinted at Mason. "Remind me to never play poker with you, son." Mason realized Driscoll was more serious than not.

"When you hold the high hand, play it to the hilt. C'mon, let's get on with the party," Mason said.

He had never danced with Laura. Dancing, in his part of Texas, included most of the Mexican dances and those of America, while at the Point he'd learned still others. Here the music was furnished by a fiddle, a guitar, and a mouth organ, and what it lacked in quality, it made up for in volume.

As it turned out, Laura was an excellent dancer, and he danced almost every dance with her—but told her the reason was that he just liked to hold her close. She came back at him with: "Don't care what your reason is, cowboy, just don't let the music stop."

Mason cut himself out a few chores in the days that followed. He helped with routine tasks around the ranch, cleaned and oiled his guns, brushed and grained the black, and did other odd jobs, until he figured he'd given all a chance to make their hands aware that he was in for the long haul—that he might need some of their help for a special task.

It took him the better part of two weeks to select the men he would have around him. All were fighting men, the kind he wanted at his back. The ranchers were told nothing except that they would find horses had been swapped in the middle of the night—and that they would see very little of their men until the score with Slade and Hamilton was settled.

There were but eight men in this salty bunch Mason selected, excluding himself. The young Mexican-American, Jaime Martinez, from the Circle T, was a happy-go-lucky puncher, but Mason saw that under Martinez's facade was pure steel. This man that everyone called friend was one of the best.

Mason had never seen Martinez use his guns, but his answer when asked if he could get them into action, fast and accurate, was a shrug and a quiet "I would not be here today, señor, if I could not."

The rest of them fit into the same category—young, tough, and loyal.

Mason had met one of them, Clint Brody, in town and recognized him as having worked off and on for Bill Hickock as a deputy. Hickock had tried to get him to stay and become a permanent law officer, but Brody didn't like the routine and had drifted.

Brody and Mason had crossed trails several times, so when Mason asked Brody to join him, Brody agreed, to Mason's surprise. This was one gun Mason knew to be both quick and accurate. He felt good about the men he had chosen.

Mason and his men were camped in a small box canyon across the valley, close to the mountains. It was away from most of the ranches and far removed from any travel trails, and far enough out of the way so that a cooking fire would not draw attention.

The fire, with a haunch of venison sizzling above it, was under the overhang of some large juniper trees so as to disperse the smoke as it drifted through the branches. The men were all hot and tired from riding, lying around in the shade, smoking and talking, with one or two catching a short siesta. Mason decided it was time he told them the details of what he had planned. They already knew some of it.

"Gather around, men. Want to palaver a bit." He sat on a fallen log. "First off, reckon there's not a one of you who don't know your brand has been losing cattle—right?"

Mason's glance showed them all nod, with the exception of Clint Brody. "Do any of you have any idea who is doing the rustling?" He chuckled at the chorus of shouted "Slade."

"Then we are agreed that the Slade bunch is responsible, and we all know there are not enough experienced guns in the valley to fight them."

Mason went on. "I have a plan, but I'll be honest with you. Some of the things we'll be doing will, in the eyes of the law, be enough to put us on the owl-hoot trail.

"I figure we have to fight fire with fire. If any of you want to back out, do it now; if not, we ride together." He looked around to see if there was any hesitation on the part of any of them. Their eyes reflected loyalty, and something else—anticipation. Each of them was looking forward to this like a boy to his first pony.

Jaime Martinez said softly, "Looks like you are stuck with all of us, señor. Ees about time we stood up straight like men and did something about the Slades. They been riding over us like we the worms." He sat back and rolled a cigarette, never taking his eyes off Mason.

"Then here is the way I have it figured," Mason said. "We can't fight the Slades in a wide-open shootout. Just aren't enough of us. We'll hurt them by hit-and-run tactics, taking a few of Slade's cattle with us each time—but in the end, it's going to come down to a shootout. When Slade, his brother, and Hamilton are dead or quit, the rest of them will drift."

A look of surprise crossed each of their faces, and Mason realized that he had not said anything, until now, about Hamilton.

"Reckon I'd better tell you how I think they are working their little game." Mason pushed his hat to the back of his head and wiped his brow. "Before I get into that I want to make something real clear. Bart Slade and Hamilton are mine. I didn't bring any of you here to get you killed.

"I figure any of you can handle Tom Slade, but those other two, well, there are probably only Clint Brody and myself who may be able to handle them, and I'm not sure either of *us* can. I'll pick the time and place that showdown will occur. Now let me tell you what they are doing, and what I believe they intend to accomplish."

They gathered closer around Mason as he detailed the picture as he saw it.

Chuck Cagle, of the Slant T, said, "Whew! Slick as a newborn calf." He swept the rest of the men with a cold look. "I'm gonna say it here an' now, I ride for the brand, an' until this little mess is wrapped up, this here bunch is my brand."

"Aw, I reckon you didn't have to say that, Chuck," Jack Rains of the B-Bar-B grunted, "but I reckon you done said it for all of us."

A chorus of approvals followed Rains's comment.

"I never doubted any of you," Mason said. "I knew when I picked you out of the fold you were of that stripe. We won't talk about that end of it anymore." He stood and said to Martinez, "You come with me. I'm going to close the sale on Hans Larsen's place. I'll need a witness." He turned to Brody.

"You're in charge while I'm gone. Break up into pairs and scout the area for a place we can hide cattle—box canyons with rock or talus approaches. You know the kind of place we need, but whatever you do, don't fight with the Slade outfit. If you see any of them, ride around them or disappear into any cover you can find. I'll see you back here tomorrow evening." He leaned over and picked up his saddle. "C'mon, Martinez, let's slope."

It was after midnight when they rode into town. A quarter moon was adding its meager light to that of the stars and showed that the hitch rails along the street were empty.

"I'm gonna bed down in the livery. If you want a room at the hotel, I'll pay," Mason said.

"No, señor. I have a pretty little señorita here that I have not seen in too long a time." Martinez smiled. "I'll meet you at the café for breakfast. Six o'clock all right?" It was.

Mason slipped in and stabled his horse, saw to it he was comfortable, then climbed into the loft. He spread his blanket and went to sleep.

The tempting smells of frying bacon and coffee brewing were Mason's first signs of a new day. He opened his eyes. It was still dark, but he heard Murtry banging a bucket around down below while feeding and watering the horses. Mason stretched, crawled out of his blankets, and climbed down.

Murtry was bent over a feed bin. He twisted his head and looked sourly at Mason. "Knew it was you. Saw your horse," he said. "A'ready fed an' watered him—helluva time a day to have to git out an' git movin'."

Mason chuckled. "C'mon, old-timer, you didn't have to get up now. It must still be a half hour till sunup."

"Aw, well I didn't have nothin' better to do," Murtry said, a grin breaking his wrinkles into more wrinkles. "What you doin' in town?"

"That coffee smells 'bout ready. I'll tell you about it over a cup."

Mason told Murtry about the meeting of the ranchers, and about Hans Larsen wanting to get out of the country. He also told him that his father had deposited some money with Wells Fargo for his use, and how he was going to buy the Larsen place. "And I'm gonna cover the mortgage notes Hamilton is carrying on the other outfits around here."

Murtry carefully poured coffee from his cup into his saucer and blew it cool, then said, "That should start the music *an'* the dancin'." He shook his head. "Boy, when you start trouble, you start it all at once, don't you?" He wasn't asking for an answer.

Mason finished his coffee and put his cup down. "Jaime Martinez is meeting me over at the café. C'mon and have breakfast with us. That bacon'll keep."

Murtry shook his head. "No, you go ahead." Then he winked at Mason. "You know how to pick 'em, boy. That Jaime Martinez is one helluva good man." He stuck out his hand. "Good luck, son."

Mason nodded his thanks, and left.

When the Larsens guided their buckboard up to the parking area in front of the livery, Mason and Martinez had had breakfast and been to the Wells Fargo office. They were ready for their visit to the bank.

"Hello, Larsen, Mrs. Larsen," Mason said. "I reckon you know Mr. Martinez."

Mason helped Mrs. Larsen, a quiet, rather pretty girl, down from the wagon. He looked from one to the other of them. "It's still not too late to change your mind about selling. I'll carry your mortgage."

"No, Mr. Mason, we've talked it over, and want to go back to Ohio," Larsen said.

"Good, let's go see Hamilton," he said, and started to turn away, then turned back. "By the way, I'll be signing those papers 'C. Charles Mason.' Just forget you ever heard me called by any other name."

"Fine by me, Mr. Mason. I never knowed you by any other name anyway."

When Hamilton saw the Larsens walk in with Mason and Martinez, his eyes went flat and cold. Mason saw at once that Hamilton was not only on his guard, but strung tight as a fiddle.

"Well, what can I do for you good people this morning?" he asked.

Larsen came right to the point. "We come in to pay off my note, Mr. Hamilton."

"Pay it off?" Hamilton looked puzzled. "It isn't due for six months yet. There's no hurry, you know."

"Maybe, but I want to pay it off now."

Hamilton turned to a file in back of his desk, rifled through several folders, pulled one out, and read.

"Ah yes, I see," he muttered, then turned back to Larsen. "You realize if you pay this off ahead of time there will be a penalty of seventy-five percent of the interest at maturity."

Larsen looked stunned. "No, sir, I didn't know that," he stammered.

Mason stepped forward, and before Hamilton could stop him, he had pulled the folder away and was looking at it.

"Here now. You have no right to see that. It's private business," Hamilton said.

"Yes I do have a right to see it. I'm buying Larsen's mortgage." Mason scanned the note quickly and saw that there was not a clause in it that provided for penalty upon early payment.

"I'm afraid you neglected to put those words into the contract, Hamilton. Reckon you might have a hard time collecting." He held the paper out in front of him. "The remaining principal is five hundred twenty-three dollars." He leaned over Hamilton's desk, filled out the Wells Fargo draft, scratched "Paid in Full" across the face of the note, and handed it to Larsen.

Mason stepped aside for the Larsens to go ahead of him. When they had cleared the office, Mason motioned Martinez out, and then nodded. "Have a nice day, Mr. Hamilton," he said. He turned and walked casually out of the bank.

7

THINGS HAD GONE well, Mason mused. He and Martinez rode toward the pocket in the hills where they'd left the rest of the men. Larsen's spread now belonged to Mason. They had signed the papers at the lawyer's office before leaving town, and the Larsens were now free to head for Ohio.

Mason twisted in his saddle and faced Martinez, a smile crinkling the corners of his eyes. "I think I made an enemy today like few men can claim. What do you think?"

Martinez looked at Mason a moment. "I theenk so, Señor Mason, but then, what would life be without a few good enemies, eh? It makes life more interesting—worth living."

The sun hot on his shoulders, Mason felt sweat trickle between his shoulder blades and down the side of his face. They rode in silence.

Heavy, dark clouds gathered around the tops of the closer mountains, hanging black above the rimrock. "We'll get some rain out of that," Mason said, nodding toward the mountains, and nudged the black to a faster pace. "Probably get wet too, but it'll be good for the grass."

Another two hours and the clouds were closer. The wind picked up and gusted hard. The smell of rain and dust permeated the air as the two riders bent their heads into the storm. Mason glanced at Martinez. "Looks like it'll be on us in another hour or so. Should be able to make it to the Larsen place before it hits. What do you think?"

"I theenk mi madre teach me to come in out of the rain eef I have the chance," Martinez said, "but you mean the *Mason* ranch, do you not, señor?" Then his face broke into a smile. "We must get used to you being the beeg ranch owner, eh?"

71

Mason slapped Martinez's horse on the rump and at the same time kneed his own horse into a run. "C'mon then, let's head for the *Mason* spread." The black took the bit and flattened out in a dead run.

They were still a couple of hundred yards from the house when the sky opened up, driving the rain into them horizontally, in sheets.

They pulled to a halt in front of the barn and led their mounts into the dry semidarkness.

After taking care of the horses, they raced for the bunkhouse since it was closest.

It was empty of riders. Mason had not expected to find any there this time of day. Larsen had only two cowhands. Mason had told them on a previous visit he wanted them to stay after he took over.

Both of them old-timers, they gladly accepted his offer. They were good, steady hands, according to Larsen, and Mason was glad to have them.

He and Martinez shucked their wet clothing and were laying a fire when Mason stopped and signaled for quiet. Horses, several of them, approached, and knowing that the hoofbeats indicated more than two horses, Mason figured the riders were not his.

He ducked and peered out a window. Martinez followed suit, looking from the adjacent window. It was still raining hard, but Mason recognized Tom Slade. Neither he nor those with him had any business here.

One of Slade's men untied a coal oil can from the side of his saddle. Mason glanced at Martinez and motioned toward their rifles.

"Do we shoot to keel, señor?"

"If we don't do it today, we'll have it to do another day." He nodded. "Yeah, put your slugs where they count."

The rider, the one with the can of coal oil, ran to the porch and started sloshing it against the walls. Mason drew a bead on his ear and squeezed off a shot. At the same time, Martinez dropped the one trying to strike a match. The rider who'd been sloshing the coal oil slammed against the wall, half of his head gone.

The one in Martinez's sights backed up and sank to the porch floor. His mouth opened and closed a couple of times before blood oozed from it and he slumped to the side.

The rest of Slade's men ran for their horses, firing blindly at the bunkhouse, obviously more interested in getting away than hitting anything. Their shots were not close.

"Let 'em go," Mason yelled above the noise of the rain hitting the tin roof. "They don't know how many they're facing. They'll get out of here fast. Didn't expect to find anyone here, judging by the way they rode up. I'd say Hamilton got word to them mighty fast. They must have been in town when we were or they couldn't have gotten here so quick."

Mason waved his hand in front of his eyes, trying to fan the thick gunsmoke away in order to see better—and get the stench of it from his nostrils.

"I theenk you ees right," Martinez said, "but I don't theenk they weel make that same meestake two times." He turned from the window, went to the bunk, and stood his rifle against it. Then he looked at the stove. "Better get that fire going."

Mason decided to stay overnight. He told Martinez to ride out in the morning, find the rest of the bunch, and bring them to the ranch. In the meanwhile he would stay put and see if he might surprise any more uninvited guests.

They slept well and woke to clear skies. The rain had washed the air sparkling clean.

After helping Mason bury the dead from the night before, Martinez saddled and rode out with the promise to be back by sundown.

Mason took the opportunity to look through the ranch house, outbuildings, and corrals. Even though Larsen professed to be a farmer with scant knowledge of cattle, he had run a tidy little spread.

The bunkhouse was fully furnished, the bunks were built in, and the large wood-burning cookstove doubled for heating and cooking. There were also three sturdy, comfortable chairs.

The Larsens had left a few odds and ends of furniture in the main house, enough, Mason judged, to get by with until he could get more.

He had also noted when he rode over the ranch, before he agreed to the price with Larsen, that the fences were in good shape. The shop, attached to the barn, had a good forge, anvil, and set of blacksmithing tools.

He leaned against the railing at the corral and allowed himself a satisfied sigh, a feeling of accomplishment. "Pa will like this," he said aloud. "I'll get *him* all the good grass and water that comes available, but the basin is mine."

He wanted his father to saddle up and come on out, but he didn't want him involved in the gunplay that would come. He decided to clean up the mess with the Slades first.

Mason wondered if part of his hesitation wasn't because his father would surely find out about his reputation. "Hell, I'm not proud of it—but I'm not ashamed of it either. I didn't ask for it, or try to get the name 'gunfighter' saddled on me," he said aloud.

There wasn't much to do. He didn't want to leave before the men arrived. Then too, there was a tightness to his gut that said he might get another visit from the Slades.

They had been bent on burning the house, and perhaps the outbuildings also, but had been surprised. Knowing they would not give up easily, Mason kept a sharp lookout for sign of riders. The one blind spot was the ravine that ran to within a hundred yards of the corral.

The day was getting hotter. He'd done no more than putter around, but had worked up a pretty good sweat; his shirt was sticking to his back, and his eyes burned as a trickle of the salty fluid found them. Wiping his brow on his sleeve, he again searched the surrounding range, paying particular attention to the area that outlined the ravine. He saw nothing.

A couple of rails on the corral fence looked a little loose, so he went to the shop and found a hammer and nails. On the way back to the corral, his gaze again swept the area. He still saw nothing out of the ordinary.

A couple of nails tightened one board, and a look at the other showed he'd been right, it also needed a couple.

He reached in his pocket for another nail, dropped it, and bent to pick it up. That was what saved him. The whine of a bullet passed where his head had been but a moment before, followed by the sharp report of a rifle.

Mason dived for the ground and came up behind the watering trough. He tried to get a line on where the shot had come from, but didn't see the glint of the sun off a rifle barrel, or a wisp of smoke. He decided it had to have come from the ravine.

He turned his head, careful not to expose any part of his body, and saw his rifle leaning against a fence post about fifteen feet away. He'd leaned it there when driving the nails. He had to get it. His handgun was not accurate over the distance he had to fire. Whoever was out there had a clear advantage. He had to take the chance.

Knowing only the general area from which the shot had come, and hoping to draw fire, Mason threw a shot in that direction.

Before the sound of his shot died out, another bullet whirred over the trough. He had what he wanted. He saw a wisp of smoke rise from behind a slight rise about a hundred yards out. He fired three quick shots in the direction of the smoke, rolled to his feet, and made a dash for the rifle.

His hand closed around the barrel just as another slug kicked bark off the side of the post. He threw himself backward. A bullet buzzed by the spot where his body had been a split second before. Mason landed on his side and rolled to get behind the trough. He made it but was now neatly pinned down.

How much ammunition did he have? He remembered reloading his guns after the Slades had tried to hit the ranch the day before. He ran his fingers around his gunbelt, checking for missing shells. All the loops were full.

He lay stretched out, thankful the trough was of a length to protect his long body. The sun got hotter. Even his Levis were soaked now, which gave them a cooling effect, but his thirst was bad. Hell, if I get thirsty enough, I'll drink out of the horse trough, he thought. A rifle slug, low on the side of the trough, cancelled that thought as the tepid water flowed from the hole.

Glancing at the sun, Mason judged about three hours had passed since the first shot. He knew there were at least three of them, from the location of the shots fired, but they couldn't get any closer until dark. A clear field of fire stretched between the horse trough and the ravine.

Mason, for the hundredth time, thought how thankful he was that Larsen had cut the tall grass away from the buildings in order to lessen the threat of a range fire burning him out.

Every few minutes one of his unseen enemies threw a shot at the trough. Mason knew they didn't have much hope of hitting him, but were letting him know they were still there.

Again, he glanced at the bunkhouse, wishing he dared take a chance on retreating to it, the closest building to him, but every time he moved, he drew a shot.

Another glance at the sun. About two-thirty or three o'clock he judged, still about four hours of daylight left, and Martinez wouldn't get back with the men until about dusk.

Mason's thirst worsened. He picked up a small pebble and put it in his mouth to make saliva flow. It was a sorry excuse for water, but better than nothing. He lay still. Patience had saved many a man's life, Mason thought, and he had plenty of that.

Another hour passed. Suddenly Mason saw a hat skylined above the edge of the embankment. He'd not fall for an old trick like that. Then a head and shoulders took form.

Moving slowly, so his movement would not draw attention, Mason brought his rifle to bear, dead center, on the man's chest and squeezed off his shot. He drew back behind the trough.

He didn't have to see whether the man fell; he knew exactly where his shot had gone. There was one less rifle against him.

Lack of patience got a man killed every time, Mason knew. Glancing over his shoulder, he again gauged the distance to the bunkhouse behind him. That son of a gun wasn't any damn closer than the last time he'd looked. He shook his head. "Patience—remember, Mason, patience," he said to himself.

The fire from the draw slacked off. They were much more careful. The sun beat mercilessly upon him, but Mason knew the Slade men were sweating just as much as he was, though they probably had canteens.

What the hell, he thought, he could stand it as long as they could, and, he reflected with some satisfaction, they were pinned down just as tightly as he was. They couldn't get any closer without exposing themselves, and showed no inclination to try.

He pulled his hat down so he could see no more than a slit of daylight above the rise behind which they were hidden. This was not the time to get sun blinded. He waited.

Another hour passed. It seemed like a week. He wondered if they would make an effort to get to their friend, to either carry him home across his saddle or give him aid if he needed it.

Mason answered his own question. Their kind had no loyalty or compassion for anyone or anything. They measured loyalty in dollars.

A head of greasy, stringy hair broke his thoughts. It raised, very slowly, until Mason had a bead, dead center, between a pair of slitted eyes. He squeezed off his shot, just as he saw the gunman's eyes widen, obviously looking down the bore of Mason's rifle.

From where Mason lay, it looked as though the man had suddenly gotten a third eye, just above and between the other two.

One left, Mason thought, and settled back to wait. It was then he heard the drum of horse's hooves, retreating fast. He stayed where he was. This too could be a trick.

He waited until the sun was full down. The sky, still bright, silhouetted the rise behind which Slade's riders had hidden.

Mason crawled from behind the watering trough, keeping his gaze on the skyline. Dragging himself along on his elbows, he covered the full hundred yards to the spot where he'd seen the last gunman. He lay his rifle down and drew his handgun.

With his left hand he picked up a rock and heaved it toward where the last man he'd shot had been lying. The second it thumped against the ground, Mason bounded over the lip of the rise.

There were only two bodies there. He holstered his .44 and walked to the bank of the ravine. Two horses stood, three-legged, their heads hanging close to the ground.

Mason gathered their reins in his left hand, still cautious. These horses needed water as badly as he did. He led them to the two who had, only a short time ago, been intent on killing him, and sighed and swallowed hard at the bile that welled into his throat. Their killing days were over. They were already drawing flies.

Someday there would be law in this raw land he loved so much, and guns would no longer be needed. "If I'm lucky," he grunted, "I'll still be around to see it."

In the waning light Mason watered the horses and dragged the bodies of the two gunmen into the barn. He would have the men bury them in the morning.

He walked to the water bucket and took the dipper off the wall. He dipped it in the water, then realized he still had the pebble in his mouth. He spat it out, swallowed a few cooling gulps, and poured the rest of the water over his head. He couldn't remember anything ever feeling so good.

Now for something to eat. It had been a long time since breakfast.

He went to the house and on back to the kitchen. When he saw the full wood bin, he grunted with satisfaction. He was dead tired. The afternoon had taken a lot out of him, but tired or no, the fire had to be built. Mason put wood and kindling in the stove and lit it, then slumped in a chair and relaxed.

The Larsens had left some staples in the cupboard. He put what he needed on the kitchen table and went out to the henhouse to gather eggs. When Martinez rode in with the men, they'd be hungry. He carefully placed the eggs in his hat. He estimated he'd gathered about three dozen.

Mason mixed a batch of biscuits and put a half dozen or so in the oven; the rest would go in when the men arrived, so as to be hot.

He finished eating, cleaned up, and went to the porch, pulling the rocker back close to the wall. He sat, leaning his rifle against the wall, within easy reach.

The evening had turned out cool, without any wind to speak of. He leaned back, willing himself to relax, letting the softness of the twilight wash the day's events from his thoughts.

Eyelids heavy, he had begun to doze when a faint drumming of horses' hooves penetrated his thoughts. He reached and picked up his rifle, only as a precaution, for he was sure it was Martinez with the rest of the men.

"Hello the house," someone yelled. Mason recognized the voice as belonging to Bob Brannigan.

"Ride on in, boys. There's a fire in the stove, coffee's on, and chuck's ready for cooking. Light and rest your saddles."

They waved to him as they passed, going directly to the stable to care for their horses. When they had finished and washed up, Mason joined them in the kitchen.

While they were eating, he filled them in on the day's events and asked Brody to have the Slade men buried in the morning.

Brody said, "Yeah. We seen yore two trophies out yonder in the stable."

Martinez finished eating, sat back, and rolled and lit a smoke. He took a long drag, then blew the smoke out slowly. "Ees not very healthy to poosh thees boss of ours, eh, vaqueros?"

"Boy, wait'll you see him draw that .44 of his," Brannigan broke in.

"Wait a minute," Mason said, "I don't need anything added to my reputation." Anger and something else—remorse maybe—washed over him.

"It is one of the worst things that can happen to a man. Every trigger-happy kid, or gunny, that comes along wants to get you in a gunfight, and that's exactly why I've been careful to keep my name from being spread around. I expect every man of you to help me keep it a secret." He looked down at the floor, then added softly, "I hate killing."

There was a moment of complete silence, then so low that they hardly caught all of the words, Martinez said, "You can trust us, señor; no one weel ever know from one of us."

"Thanks, men." Mason said. "Now let's look at how we figure to operate. First, we'll stay here as long as it's healthy. We'll split up. Some will sleep here in the house, some in the bunkhouse, and some in the barn. We won't get trapped in a cross fire."

He went on, "Now about this box canyon you found. Some of us will ride out and take a look. We'll drag brush, or whatever's available, across the mouth so as to close it off.

"We'll all ride Slade's range and haze any strays we see toward the canyon. By the way," he said, looking at Chuck Cagle of the Slant T, "you found this place. About how many head will it hold, and how long would the grass and water hold out if we filled it with cattle?"

Cagle scratched his head and said, "Oh, I reckon maybe a couple thousand head, for 'bout three months or so." He nodded to himself more than to anyone else. "Yep, I'd say that's a purty good reckon."

"Good," Mason cut in. "We start tomorrow, and if you see anyone—any rider, Slade's or otherwise—break off what you're doing and disappear. Don't want anyone knowin' what we're doing. Unbranded stuff we'll brand, divided equally among the outfits represented here. Now, let's get some sleep."

He said to Brody, "Set a night watch, one man at a time. Don't want any more surprises."

8

MASON HUNKERED CLOSER to the fire. It was still early September, but in this high country the air already had a chill to it. Fall was not far off. He squinted at the distant mountains. Several months had passed since he and his men had moved into the Larsen place. Things had gone smoothly.

They had gathered about fifteen hundred head of cattle and had them safely hidden in the canyon. They had taken only a few head at a time and had frequent enough rainfall to keep the tracks washed out. The problem now was feed.

The fall roundup had begun, and Mason knew from the count that many of the yearlings they had in the canyon belonged to the ranchers. He wanted to return them to their rightful owners.

He knew how he was going to do it, and it was inviting trouble. He would have to cross the corner of Slade's ranch, and that might take some doing. It was time he rode to the Circle B, and have Bryson set things up. The ranchers would now have to take an active part, with men—and guns—if necessary.

He told the men what he was going to do, that none of them were to leave the canyon, and to permit no one else to enter. "The dog work's about over and the ball's ready to start. Take extra care. Don't want anyone hurt unless we can't help it." He saddled up and rode out.

When he rode into the Circle B ranch yard, Curt Tilghman gave him a wave. "Howdy, Mason." He greeted him as though he had just seen him the day before. When Mason got to the house, Bryson's greeting was a little stronger.

"Where the hell you been, boy? We've been worried about you. Laura wanted to send out a search party, but I kept telling her that if anything happened one of your boys would let us know."

"Hey! Hold up there, Bryson." Mason flinched under the pounding Bryson gave his back. "I figured it best to stay away because of the danger that Slade would tie you in to the disappearance of his cattle, and maybe attack you or the ranch."

He looked past Bryson's shoulder and saw Laura standing with flour up to her elbows, and a little smudge of it on the tip of her nose. "Hi, Laura, you baking me a pie?" he quipped, but the hoped-for smile didn't appear. Instead she gave him a very cool, "Hello."

"Is that any way to greet an old friend?"

"An old friend," she said, "would have dropped by to visit once in a while."

He saw her eyes suddenly turn to green fire.

"Where have you been, Cole Mason? I've been worried sick about you, and now you show up like you haven't even been gone."

He shuffled from one foot to the other, then went over and reached up kiddingly to flick the flour from her nose, but suddenly she was in his arms.

"There, there, little girl, don't cry—please," he said, smoothing her hair back from her face. "I wouldn't do anything to bring even one tear to those pretty eyes. I just thought it best not to attract any more danger to you all here than I could help."

He was holding her close, and was aware that she wasn't a little girl, but a full-blown woman. She was beautiful, desirable, and a hundred miles out of his reach, until the valley's problems were settled.

He took his arms from about her and pulled out his handkerchief to dry her tears. It was then he noticed that Bryson had left the room.

"Pa never could stand to see me cry," Laura sniffled by way of explanation. "But I only cry when I'm mad."

Mason couldn't think of anything to say that wouldn't get her dander up, and he didn't want her to start crying again, so he suggested that they get some coffee and sit in the kitchen, where she could watch her pies.

"You only want to sit in here so I'll have to give you a slice." Laura's eyes sparkled through the tears.

Bryson came back in the kitchen and poured himself a cup of coffee.

"You young people settle your differences?" he asked, with more concern than Mason thought necessary, until he saw the twinkle in Bryson's eyes.

While he was eating the more than generous wedge of apple pie Laura put in front of him, he questioned Bryson as to whether he, or any of the ranchers, had had any gun trouble with the Slade bunch since he'd been gone.

"No, no gun trouble, but we're still losing cattle," Bryson said. "I reckon, all told, me and the other ranchers have lost eight, maybe nine hundred head, mostly yearlings. . . ."

"All right. We have about fifteen hundred head. We've branded them and are ready to bring them home. As a matter of fact, we're gonna have to move 'em soon. The grass they're on is getting mighty thin."

"When the others find out their herds haven't shrunk, maybe even grown a little, they'll smile again." Bryson hugged Laura to him with one brawny arm. "I reckon those extra cows'll help make up for those we've lost in the past."

Mason polished off the last bite of pie and held his plate out to Laura for another slice. She snorted in disbelief. He said to Bryson, "That brings us to the problem we face now. We need hands who can handle a rifle to help with the drive.

"To get them back on home range, we'll have to cross a corner of Slade's grass, maybe three miles of it, which with hard driving we should be able to cover in three or four hours."

"That's no problem," Bryson said, "Most ranch hands can handle a rifle. In fact, they're pretty good with them—handguns, no."

"If its all right with you then, I'll send Tilghman to the other ranches for trail hands. I'll meet them at the Snake ranch. I stopped by on the way here and told Sisson to expect us. His brand is the closest one to where we're holding the herd. I'll bunk down here tonight." He leaned back in his chair and smiled at Bryson. "Unless you reckon Miss Laura might run me off."

"You just keep on, Cole Mason." Laura looked at him, a warning in her eyes. "You ain't seen nothin' yet."

The day waned. The talk and the company gave Mason the atmosphere he needed to relax. He seldom experienced the closeness of friends, and he liked the feeling. He told them he'd bought the Larsen spread, but that it was really for his father. He didn't tell them about the basin. He wanted to surprise Laura with it, wanted to experience the look on her face when she first saw it.

"Sounds like you figure on staying in these parts," Bryson said.

Mason was aware that Laura looked at him intently, waiting for his answer. "A herd of wild horses couldn't drag me out of here. If Pa doesn't want Larsen's place, I'll take it." He saw Laura's face glow as though a light had been turned on in her soul.

"I've found what I've been looking for all my life. I don't think I've been aware of the constant search, but it was there. The land and weather are the best I've seen.

"You people here in the valley seem to have accepted me as one of you, and I want to build something for my children, and their children." He felt his face turn hot and knew it must be showing red, even through his sun-browned skin. He felt the need to say something more. "I reckon to do that if I find a girl who'll have me."

They talked for a while longer; then Mason excused himself and bid them good night. Bryson wanted him to stay in the ranch house, but Mason wanted to talk to Tilghman, so he told Bryson he'd stay in the bunkhouse. Laura walked out with him.

"Cole, this business with Slade is all coming to a head pretty soon, isn't it?"

"Yes. He hasn't made a drive since I've been here. His men are probably getting restless, and my guess is he's needing the money pretty bad by now." He stopped and faced her. "Yep, it's coming to a head right soon. I want you to promise me something—keep your father out of it."

"You know I can't promise that, Cole. If he knows when and where it's going to happen, he'll be there." She placed her hand on his forearm. "It's already gnawing at him that you are fighting everyone else's fight. He's worried for you, Cole. Somehow he's gotten to think of you almost as a son."

"I appreciate that, Laura. I like him too, but . . . don't you go thinking of me as a brother."

"Don't you worry about that, you big brute."

"I'll do all I can to keep your pa in the dark. He'll know when because I'll need men, but he won't know where." He reached out and took her shoulders in his big hands. "Good night now, little girl. I'll see you again in a few days, and there's something special I want to show you when we both have the time."

"Vaya con dios, Cole," Laura whispered so softly that he barely heard.

When he explained what he intended doing, and how, Tilghman wanted to be part of it, but Mason said no. "You'll be needed here, and your biggest job'll be to keep Bryson with you so he'll not try to join up with the drive. The way I've got it planned. No one should get hurt, but there's always that chance. Keep him out of it."

"Damn, Mason, I'll swap jobs with you." Tilghman pulled a Durham sack from his pocket and twirled a cigarette. "I'd rather try to rope a grizzly than try to keep the boss out of what's comin'."

"Nevertheless, do it. If that man got hurt on account of my doings, don't reckon I'd ever forgive myself."

"I'll do it, you know I will."

"As soon as you and Bryson get me ten trail hands, we'll start. In the next couple of days I'm gonna do some scouting around. I want to be sure I'm right about the trail the Slades use to get cattle out of the valley. I'll come back by here and pick up the hands you get for me—and be damned certain they're good with a rifle. I'm gonna get some sleep."

The early morning was chilly when Mason saddled and rode from the Circle B, the sun not yet up. His intent was to circle the southeast quadrant of the valley for sign of large numbers of cattle having been driven over it. Without proof, or any clue that such a trail existed, he was groping in the dark. But it had to exist. No one had ever seen the herd moved, which meant the exit from the valley, used by the Slade gang, had to be close to Slade's ranch. That nailed it down to the southeast quarter.

Staying below the crests of hills, and using *arroyos secos,* as the Mexicans called these dry water courses, Mason worked his way toward the area in which he was sure there was a trail out of the valley. He rode with the thong off his right-hand .44

and his Winchester across the saddle horn, not wanting trouble, but ready if it came.

The mountains showed no sign of rain. He kept a wary eye on them. Any clouds hanging over their peaks and he'd vacate the arroyos. He'd seen times when it was clear overhead, and without warning, a wall of water came rushing down these dry waterways, sweeping all in front of it, the water coming from rains high in the mountains.

Toward nightfall he looked for a place to spread his bedroll. He'd have no fire, which meant no coffee or hot food. What the hell, he thought, that's the way it had to be, and without a fire, he'd make camp on higher ground, just in case there was rain on the upper slopes.

Mason rode in under a tall ponderosa pine. He stripped his horse, picketed him, and unrolled his bedroll, then sat chewing on a piece of jerky.

This was the time of day he liked, the day sounds getting bedded down and the night sounds not yet come alive. And the fresh smell of dried grass and the scent of pine off the ridges didn't stop spreading just because the sky had darkened.

The mountains turned from a deep purple to a misty gray, then were lost in a black void. Mason slid down, put his head against his saddle, and pulled his blanket up.

Slade's ranch was behind him now; he'd passed it during the false dawn and with luck could ride farther into the foothills before daylight. He'd ride easier then, and if spotted, he would have as good a play against them as they had against him.

By mid-morning he was in the higher swell of the hills; one reared its rounded top a couple thousand feet above the valley floor. Mason, thinking the trail he was seeking would not be over a hill of that size, skirted it; then he saw a trail, well worn and deep. A lot of cattle had passed this way, but he saw no sign of recent use. He was sure this was what he was looking for. And he felt certain the trail would lead to the exit from the valley.

The old trail was not hard to follow, so he spent most of his time scanning the surrounding terrain, looking for, but hoping not to find, any indication he'd been seen.

The trail led directly toward the mountain. Wondering who would drive a herd across a hill of that size, he was upon it almost before seeing it; the opening to the canyon slanted off at such an angle that he'd ridden to the canyon's mouth before being aware he'd found what he was seeking. The well-beaten trail turned and followed the canyon.

At first look the steep walls showed no path by which they could be scaled. Mason reined his horse in and studied the deep cleft. He still saw no way that a man and horse, once in the canyon, could get out, other than at its ends.

"Old hoss, if there's a rifleman on that rim, you and I will be an easy target with damned little chance of fighting back." His gaze once again swept the sides and rim of the canyon.

He nodded. "All right, let's see what we can find." A slight pressure from his knees nudged his horse into a slow walk, but despite using his customary caution, Mason felt the hair on his neck stiffen and wondered what was wrong with him.

It wasn't the feeling that he was being watched; that feeling usually tightened the muscles between his shoulders. Whatever his senses were telling him, he paid attention. A man didn't ignore this kind of warning and stay alive.

The black was skittish, jumpy. He danced to the side, apparently trying to sidestep his shadow. "Now, I've got you nervous, old black horse. Don't pay me any mind. Reckon I've been in so much trouble lately I'm dodging ghosts."

The words didn't make him feel better. Mason knew there was something he should be seeing—or doing. But what? He thought to turn the black and get out of the canyon. Whatever it was had to be in there because he'd not had the feeling until riding into its mouth.

He looked at the hoof-pounded floor of the canyon, glanced at the steep cliffs on each side, and shrugged. No, he thought, I'm not leaving. I came to see where the cows get out of the valley, and that's what I'm going to do.

His horse sidestepped, danced, and tossed his head, but Mason urged him ahead, ducked his head to ride under an overhang of rock—and saw a fast-traveling shadow cross the trail in front of him.

He threw himself to the side. He grabbed for his rifle and left the saddle at the same time. His grab missed the rifle.

He hit the ground, rolled, and faced the biggest mountain cat he'd ever seen. His horse had bolted down canyon. Mason grabbed for his .44. It was not in his holster. All he had now was his Bowie knife and his throwing knife.

In a lightning move, his hand went to the back of his neck and pulled and threw the slim blade at the cat, who crouched to spring. The knife caught him in the neck—and didn't even slow him down.

As soon as his throwing knife was in the air, Mason had repeated the motion and pulled his Bowie. It came to his hand just in time for him to catch the cat in midair. He buried it in the animal's tawny side. The monster's weight fell on him, accompanied by slashing claws. Mason hit the ground under the cat.

The cougar straddled him, front paws raking his shoulders. Mason pulled the knife from the cat's side and swung again, and again—and again, while with his left hand he tried to keep the giant teeth from his throat. He heaved upward and pushed the cat to the side. Free of the weight, Mason rolled and swayed to his feet. He was losing blood, and the claw marks along his shoulders burned and pained like nothing he'd ever experienced before.

The golden beast crouched in front of him, shook his head, trying to throw the knife out of his neck, and then crouched low to the ground, readying for another spring.

When the beast left the ground, Mason sidestepped and swung and buried his Bowie to the hilt just behind the cat's shoulder. That stabbing thrust had to be the one to do it— because Mason now had no ready weapon. His left hand .44 was thonged down. A cluster of boulders at the base of the cliff drew his attention. His eyes not leaving the cat, Mason edged toward the nearest boulder.

The cougar hit the ground, rolled, and squalled, trying to get the knives out. Then giving it up, he crouched on his stomach, shook his head, and tried to muster his strength for another spring. All Mason had left were his fists. He'd never tried to knock out a hundred-and-fifty pound cat before, but it was his only choice now.

Mason crouched by the big rock, ready to swing from the ground with everything he had. The cat looked at him, his golden eyes spitting hate.

He dug his claws into the ground's granite surface, readying to spring. The claws raked back, but failed to launch the cat. He fell forward, head stretched toward Mason. The cougar lay there, took a breath that swelled its sides, and died.

Mason glanced at his shoulders and arms. Deep gouges showed through his shredded shirt, from shoulders to wrists. He took a long, shuddering breath, and then fear washed over him.

Before retrieving his knives, he walked to a large boulder and sat, letting the sickness of fear empty his stomach, letting the weakness of it take him. He stared at the ground, allowing waves of gut-wrenching horror wash over him until he was drained of all emotion.

Finally he raised his gaze, realizing he'd been staring at one rock, for how long he didn't know. He looked at the giant cat. In death, it didn't seem to be the awesome, fearful creature he'd fought.

Mason stood, walked to the side of the cougar, and withdrew his knives. Then, using the Bowie, he cut off a haunch and skinned the animal, keeping its head intact. After rolling the head in the pelt, he looked for his horse. It was nowhere to be seen.

Pushing his hat to the back of his head, Mason wiped perspiration from his brow, thinking back over what had happened when he'd launched himself from his saddle. If I remember right, he thought, that old black horse ran off down canyon. He nodded. Reckon I might have a long walk. If he was as scared as I was, he's probably still making tracks.

He stashed the cougar pelt under some rocks, and it was then he remembered that his handgun had been missing when he reached for it. A glance about the area, and he saw where it had fallen from his holster. His left handgun was still snug against his thigh, held in place by the hammer thong.

"That's one time being ready to draw damned near cost me my life," he said, remembering that he'd slipped the thong from his right-hand gun in case a Slade rider surprised him on the trail.

Mason picked up his gun and blew the dirt from it. He turned and headed down the canyon.

Between the canyon walls the heat was suffocating, and he had no water. His shoulders and arms pained worse now. As bad as he wanted a drink, he wanted to wash out his wounds more. Infection could put him down for a while, and the schedule he'd set for moving the cows would not stand delay.

Sweat drenched his shirt. He stopped again to mop his brow, wishing he had his moccasins. His feet were getting sore; boots were not made for walking. Settling his hat back firmly on his head, he set out again, rounded a boulder—and there stood the black, his head held to the side to keep from stepping on the trailing reins.

"Old hoss, don't reckon I was ever so glad to see anybody as much as I am you." Mason walked to his horse and reached for the reins. The black shied, apparently smelling the blood. "Whoa up now, there's nothing to be afraid of. I took care of what you were trying to tell me about. That cat's dead as last week's news."

He gathered the reins and, holding them in one hand, looked the horse over for scratches he might have gotten when the cat sailed by. His back and flanks had not a scratch on them. Mason mounted, thinking the sensible thing to do would be to head for the ranch and get his wound attended to. To hell with it, he thought, he'd not used good sense right along or he wouldn't be here trying to help people that he didn't owe a red cent. He reached out and patted the black. Nope, he thought, don't owe them a damn thing, but reckon you don't have to owe folks in order to want to help them. A little knee pressure, and he headed the horse on down the canyon.

When they came out the other end, Mason saw more sign that great numbers of cattle had moved through there. The ground was softer and the hooves had cut deeply into it. The trail he looked at would be discernible for a long time.

His wounds needed attention, now, not in a couple of days. Mason thought to use bacon fat on them, then decided it wouldn't do much good unless they were festering.

Seeing a large pine to the side of the trail, he wondered if pine sap might not keep infection from setting in. Well why not? he thought. They make turpentine from it. Hell, gotta try something.

Luckily, the pine had been scored down two sides, and sap oozed from the scratches in its bark. A good-sized bear fixed that tree for us, Mason thought. Don't reckon I'd like to meet up with him though. Reckon I've had about all that kind of fun I can stand for one day.

He dismounted and peeled the sap, still soft, from the scratches. Then, spreading the sides of the claw marks apart, he stuffed the soft rosin into them. He'd not gone far with the job before he realized he'd have to stand about as much pain as he'd ever known. The sap burned like a million branding irons. Before finishing, he stopped twice to keep from passing out. As soon as the weakness passed, he continued to tamp the rosin into the raw, open wounds.

Finished, he sat leaning against the bole of the tree, sweat streaming down his face. He squeezed his eyes tightly shut, trying to stifle the pain, which seemed to wash over him in waves, and to last forever. It finally subsided into a constant, throbbing ache. He mounted and went back into the canyon.

Riding back through it, Mason planned how he'd stop the next trail drive the Slades made. When satisfied that his plan would work, he thought, It'll be inhuman, but that's what we're gonna do.

He camped in the canyon that night, figuring to have a fire, coffee, and hot food. The cluster of boulders in which he'd chosen to spread his groundsheet would also hold the firelight from sight.

When he'd finished supper and scoured his mess gear with sand, Mason lay down to try and sleep. It didn't come easy; every position he tried seemed to put pressure on claw cuts. When he was about ready to give up, saddle his horse, and ride on, sleep came.

Opening his eyes a slit, and not knowing how long he'd slept, Mason lay still, getting the feel of his surroundings. Then he tightened his muscles to stand.

Hot, burning knives seemed to pierce every inch of his shoulders and arms. He relaxed, pushing his head hard against his saddle, bracing for the pain that wouldn't stop.

Then, knowing he couldn't lie there forever, he bunched his muscles, gritted his teeth, and pushed to his feet. He stood still, letting the pain wash over him. Not only the claw cuts hurt, but it seemed that every bone in his body was bent on causing more pain.

Thought I was in pretty good shape he said to himself. Reckon that cat forced me to use moves and muscles I hadn't used in years. The way I feel I'm sure as hell not gonna use 'em again soon.

A small fire warmed some of the stiffness from him. The rest of his water went into the coffee, which, with a haunch he'd cut from the cat and seasoned with bacon, and a tin of beans, made up his breakfast.

Moving about the camp, saddling and getting ready to ride, worked most of the stiffness from his muscles, but did nothing toward making his wounds feel better. The black gave him some trouble when he tied the cougar pelt behind his saddle, but after shying to the side a couple of times, he settled down and let Mason tie it in place.

Finally, he mounted and rode toward Bryson's ranch.

Only once during his ride did he see another human and that was from a distance. He'd kept out of sight, letting the rider disappear before he rode on.

When he reached the ranch yard, there were close to twenty horses there that didn't wear Bryson's brand, so Mason knew Tilghman had done his job.

Despite Laura's attempt to keep him under her care until his wounds healed, he gathered the men and headed for the box canyon.

Mason counted on the Slades to stay clear of the drive. He had ten good hands, plus his eight men, all with rifles. He thought that unless the Slades could get in close, close enough for handgun work, they'd stay away, because a pitched battle with rifles wouldn't be to their liking.

He was riding point when Tilghman joined up with the herd. Mason had tried to make him stay with Bryson, but it didn't work, and he had to admit he was glad to have another rifle.

"If any Slade people try to come in on us, have your rifles clear of leather but don't fire unless they are bent on a fight. I don't believe they'll force one on us with the odds so close," he yelled above the trail noise. "All right, fall back with the herd and let's keep 'em moving."

Mason rode warily. He kept a sharp lookout along the ridges. They were about an hour onto Slade's range when he saw a rider top the ridge to his right. He watched him ride along it long enough to estimate the size of the herd and the number of riders; then he reined his horse back down the other side.

They know we're here, Mason thought. "Now we'll see what they're made of."

The sun beat down, and even with the more than adequate rains, the dust boiled up around the herd, choking cattle and riders alike. Mason rode off to the side for a look. The cattle were tightly bunched, just as he wanted them, and they were moving well.

He wasn't concerned about weight loss, so he had his riders push the herd faster than on a long trail drive. These cattle were not being driven to market.

He watched his riders. They cast searching glances along the ridges and then turned their attention back to the herd. Mason nodded approval, then reined his horse toward the rear of the herd, where he knew he would find Tilghman riding drag. Tilghman took the dirty jobs right along with the rest of the crew.

Finally, Mason made him out, a vague ghostlike figure in the roiling dust. "Tilghman," he shouted above the din of cattle hooves and impatient lowing and the yelling of the riders as they kept the cattle bunched. "Tilghman, I'm gonna drop back for a look-see. If anything should happen, you take charge." At Tilghman's nod, Mason faded into the dust of the backtrail.

He didn't expect anything to happen, but he knew he was a marked man. There wasn't a man in the valley Slade wanted dead more than him, so he rode with more than his usual caution. Even with that he was only fifteen or twenty yards from them before he was aware of it. There were seven of them, all Slade men, and they saw him at the same time.

The front rider grabbed for his gun. Suddenly Mason was firing. They all filled their hands and returned his fire. The foremost riders pulled up and tried to rein their horses back. The horses got tangled and threw their riders' aim off. Had it not been for that, Mason knew his worries about the valley would have been over.

Two riders went down. At the same time Mason felt a searing pain low in his side and knew he'd been hit. He dug spurs into the black and was in the middle of them. He fired point-blank into a rider in front of him, then fired to the side as he was about through the bunch.

Two more went down, and the remaining three broke free, gouged spurs into their horses, and headed down the backtrail. Mason methodically thumbed his hammer back and squeezed the trigger, then realized the shots he heard were not his own. His guns were empty.

Tilghman and Brody were kneeling in the dust, their rifles spewing flame. Then the world tilted, and Mason saw the ground come up to meet him.

It seemed to Mason that he was swimming in a great black sea. He'd almost reach the top, where there was light, and voices; then he would sink again. Finally, when it seemed that he would surely drown if he went down one more time, he reached the surface.

Everything was pain. "Must have hit a rock," he mumbled, then opened his eyes, just a slit. He was not in a sea at all, but in bed in a room he'd never seen. It was all right though, because Laura sat in a rocker beside his bed. She was sound asleep. Mason closed his eyes. The sea was gone and he slept.

He tried to wake several times. He didn't know how long, or how many times, he tried, but he finally opened his eyes.

It was a bright, shiny morning he awoke to, and Laura was sitting there, just as he had somehow known she was, even when he couldn't get his eyes open to the world. He didn't know whether he had dreamed it, but he thought she'd been holding his hand while talking to him.

"Oh, Cole, my love, hang on, get well for me. Fight, Cole, fight. Make this a good fight—for us." She was still talking; only he couldn't hear the rest of it. But he knew one thing for sure—dream or no dream, he was going to get well.

He turned his head and looked at her. The crystal brightness of the morning was dim when compared with her smile. "Welcome back, Cole," was all she said. Her eyes said the rest.

"Thirsty—an' I could eat a horse," Mason whispered through cracked, fever-parched lips.

"Well, now!" Laura said and squeezed his hand. "I would say you must be getting well." She stood. "I'll go fix you something."

"Wait . . ." Cole glanced around the room. "Where am I? This isn't the Circle B. What happened to me? I remember taking a hit in the side, but not much else."

"You're at the Snake, and we'll talk about the rest when you're stronger. Now you just lay quiet while I get your breakfast. Then I'm going to get some sleep."

The days were warm and sunny, the nights cold and crisp. Fall was in the air. Mason gained strength, and itched to get back in the saddle.

Sam Sisson, the owner of the Snake, told him he'd taken four slugs, and that three of them had gone all the way through. He had taken one high in the chest, but fortunately it had missed his lungs, heart, and major arteries. It was the one that put him down. The others: One in the thigh, they had to dig that slug out; one in the left side, it was the one he'd felt; and one that had grazed his ribs.

Tilghman had taken charge of the herd and seen to it that each rancher got his cut. Brody and Martinez had gone ahead of the herd with Mason tied to a travois.

Sisson, an old bachelor, had turned his ranch house over to Laura once she arrived.

She had not left Mason's side but a few minutes at a time during the two weeks in which he fought off death.

According to Tilghman, she had dragged him back from the divide several times by holding his hand and talking steadily to him.

Now that he was mending, she was still with him. She sat with him, walked with him, and all the while talked to him, guiding him into the things to do so he would properly mend. The Slades were ominously quiet.

Mason wondered what Slade's next move would be. The ranchers were busy with roundup, and this would leave a goodly area of each ranch unprotected.

The trail drive gunfight had served to notify Slade, and probably Hamilton, that the ranchers were through being bullied. Now Mason expected them to start the harrying types of moves so typical of this sort of deal, moves to keep the ranchers off-balance, trying to guess where their men would be most useful. He expected rustling to increase, along with burned haystacks, men sniped at, and anything else that would cause problems.

Each day Mason added to the things he'd done the previous day, partly to get his body back in shape, but also to feel that in some measure he was earning his keep. Sisson insisted he stay until he was fit to ride, rope, and, if need be, to fight.

Laura mentioned going home, and Sisson pitched a fit. He said he needed Laura to help him care for Mason. Mason thought he knew the real reason.

"You know why Sisson won't hear of you leaving?" He slanted a look at Laura. They were taking their usual after-dinner walk.

"No, I really can't understand. He seems to almost get angry when either of us mentions leaving."

"You know what I think. I think he's lonesome." Mason stopped and turned to face her. He was serious, a frown creasing his brow. "Uh-huh, that's what I think. You know he's never had a wife and children, and now he's getting old. He's taken a pretty strong liking to us. Almost acts like our pa, and he hates to think of his house being empty.

"His hands are usually out and about the ranch. He has probably never had anyone he could just sit and talk with at noon, or in front of the fire at night, and now that he has experienced it, he doesn't want to give it up."

Mason turned and walked ahead, slowly. "He's been so good to me, I wouldn't hurt him for the world. I'll try to come up with something that'll satisfy him. Maybe your father won't mind if you spend some time visiting over here."

He looked at her across his shoulder and smiled. "Probably the only thing he'd miss if you didn't come around, though, would be those apple pies you make."

"Yes, you big animal, and I'm beginning to believe that's the only reason you're staying." There was just a hint of disappointment in her voice.

Mason stopped and turned toward her. He took her by the shoulders and gently pulled her to him. Her head tilted toward his; her lips parted slightly.

He lowered his lips to hers. She responded to his kiss as though she couldn't get enough. He drank in her nectar, feeling her body melt against his. It took more willpower than he thought possible, but he pushed her from him. They were both breathless.

"I . . . I never intended that to happen until I could promise you a lifetime of safety, and security." He spread his hands helplessly. "I can't do that yet."

"I intended it to happen whenever, and if ever, you wanted it to, Cole Mason. Don't I have anything to say about what happens between us?" she whispered.

"I love you, Laura. Reckon I have ever since you gave me hell after the Apache fight. I want you to be my bride, but not until this is over and done with. Besides, I have to talk with your pa. He might not like the idea of you being married to me."

"You go ahead and talk with him," she said, then chuckled. "But, I told him soon after we met that you were my man, and if you'd have me I was going to marry you." She then laughed out loud, joyously.

Mason thought her laugh must have been because of the dumbfounded look he knew was spread across his face.

"Why . . . well," he stammered, "you must have known as soon as I did."

"Cole, I knew I loved you almost from the beginning. I'm only surprised that you didn't know. Everything I did shouted it to the world. Curt knew. We talked about it. Pa knew. He asked me about it. He likes you, Cole, and I love you, so you talk to Pa."

"First, and yes I'm well enough to do it, we're going for a ride. It'll take us overnight, so we better tell Sisson. I have something special to show you."

"What, Cole, what do you have to show me?"

"Oh no, you're not going to wheedle this out of me. You'll see when we get there."

They told Sisson they were going to be gone for about two days and would be leaving early the next morning.

"Now you young'uns'll be coming back, won't you?" Sisson asked hopefully, almost pitifully.

Mason and Laura exchanged glances. "Yeah, old-timer, we'll be back by sundown day after tomorrow," Mason said. Sisson was such a big, brawny, independent cuss, Mason thought; it made him ashamed to be able to read his vulnerability. He'd never hurt Sisson on purpose, but he and Laura had to make this ride alone.

9

THE SUN WAS still an hour high when they reached the escarpment and turned to ride along its base.

"Where *are* we going, Cole? There's nothing here but talus slides and rock."

"Well, maybe I found gold, or maybe a frisky new colt, or even a wild rose," he said. "Whoa now." He pulled the black to a halt. "This is where I have to blindfold you."

"Cole Mason, you're not putting a blindfold on me."

"Aw, c'mon, Laura, it'll only be for a few minutes, and it'll spoil the surprise if you don't let me do it."

"Oh, all right, if it means that much to you, but I can't see anything for miles that could surprise me."

"You just wait," Mason said, and took his neckerchief from around his neck. Then, he carefully folded it and tied it around Laura's head, making certain it covered her eyes. Then he kissed her cheek. "I'll lead our horses carefully, so don't feel nervous."

He had watched their backtrail throughout the ride, and knew no one had followed them. They rode along the base of the escarpment a few more minutes, then turned back into the fold of granite. It was already night in the passage. Their horses' hooves made no sound as they trod the sandy path into the basin.

"It's so quiet, Cole, and I have the feeling that it's quite dark suddenly. When will we be where you are taking me?"

"Only a few more minutes," Cole answered. Then they were riding out into the basin.

"All right, now keep your eyes closed," he directed, and turned her horse so that she faced toward the lake, then slipped the blindfold from her eyes.

"Oh!" she gasped after a moment of complete silence. "Oh, it's magnificent, beautiful."

"Sounds like you like it, honey." His smile was tender. "You do, don't you?"

"Oh, you don't have to ask me that, but where is it? What is it? I've never seen it before, yet it can't be too far from where you blindfolded me."

He felt a lump swell in his throat at Laura's reaction.

"It isn't very far—yet it's a whole world away from anything we know—but one question at a time. I found it by accident. I don't believe any man has been in here in many thousands of years." He swung his leg over his horse's rump and dismounted, then helped Laura down. "We'll camp here tonight and I'll tell you about it."

Grasping the reins of both horses, he led them to the place he'd stopped before, helped Laura down, and proceeded to set up camp.

He threw more wood on the fire to ward off the evening chill. He had collected enough to last the night while Laura prepared supper. Now, with supper over, they leaned back against their saddles, sipping coffee. Mason felt at peace: his woman beside him, a warm fire.

"How would you like to have our home here?" he questioned, cocking an eyebrow.

"Do you mean it, Cole? But how? Who owns it? Maybe they won't sell."

"While I was spending time to learn all I could about the valley, I rode down to Santa Fe. I wanted to see how many, and who, of the ranchers actually owned their land, or if they were grazing government land."

He leaned over and filled Laura's cup as well as his own. "While I was there," he continued, "I checked to see who owned this basin. It turned out to be government land. I sent Pa a wire to get it for me.

"Pa has pretty strong connections in Washington. He managed to wrap it up for me, and it's every inch yours and mine." He hunkered lower against his saddle and looked off into the darkness across the basin.

"You know what, Laura, I don't believe I'll ever put cattle in here. We'll run our herd on the Larsen place, and any additional grass we can get at the right price, but this belongs to the deer, antelope, bear, and even the big cats that make their home up on the rocks. I want to leave it like it is, except for our home.

"Those who were here before didn't violate this land, and as far as I can figure, there hasn't been anyone here since before the last ice age. We'll not be the first to destroy it."

Laura looked him straight in the eyes. She said nothing for a long, quiet moment, then said, "God bless you, Cole; you're a good man. This is a Garden of Eden, our Garden of Eden, and when we're married I'd like to spend our honeymoon here, before we let anyone know about it or see it."

"That's the way it'll be then."

Laura held her hand toward him; he took it and held it until the fire faded to glowing embers. Hating to break the magic of the night, he finally stood and checked that the bed he'd prepared for Laura was comfortable enough, waited for her to crawl between the blankets, and pulled them close about her shoulders. Then he walked to the other side of the fire and slipped into his own blankets.

Mason woke Laura before dawn, wanting her to experience the coming of day in this wondrous place. He'd started the fire and made coffee when she looked up at him. He was surprised she didn't immediately raise hands to her hair and exclaim how horrible she must look. She smiled instead. "It'll not be this way after we're married. I'll have coffee ready for *you* then."

"You just stay as pretty as you are now, and I'll make it forever."

"Don't say anything you'll be sorry for later. I just might hold you to it, Cole." She laughed and threw the covers off.

The morning was all Mason could ask for. It was just as beautiful as the one he'd experienced alone here. Laura sat close and drank her coffee while watching the changing light and the unveiling of the basin as it emerged from the mist.

After long moments, she broke the silence. "May I name our paradise, Cole?"

With a smile, he nodded. "Somehow, I think any name you give it will be fitting. Yes. Do it. Tell me what you've named it, because I know you've already done so in your mind."

She giggled. "I'll have to be careful, you're getting to know me too well when you can read my mind." She drank the last of her coffee and tossed the dregs. "All right, I'll tell you. What do you think of our naming it Misty Glen?"

"Yes. It's a beautiful name you've given it." He stood. "Bad as I hate to, we'd better get on back or Sisson will think we've gone off and left him."

He saddled the horses and tied on their bedrolls, and they mounted, and rode from Misty Glen toward the Snake.

It was a full day's ride, and the sun was sinking slowly below the cloud-shrouded peaks when they rode into the ranch yard.

Laura went to the house to tell Sisson they were back, and safe, while Mason took care of the horses.

He felt good. Two days in the saddle had left him only moderately sore. It was time he took Laura home, and time for him to return to the Larsen place.

He told Sisson and Laura during supper that it was time for him and his men to do something, he wasn't sure what, to force Slade and Hamilton to show their hand. A large scale raid on Slade's herd would do no more than the raid he planned for when Slade started his trail drive, and it would cost lives. He would not unnecessarily jeopardize his men.

Sisson suggested that the trail drive raid would be enough, and Mason thought about it a moment, then agreed that it might be.

Sisson was disappointed that they were leaving, but said he knew it had to be done.

Laura was visibly upset. Mason knew it was because of what lay ahead, but . . . well, he was not a man given to riding around trouble. It was his way to meet it head-on.

Their ride to the Circle B was uneventful and comfortable. They rode most of the way in silence. A nice view would appear, or a big buck, or maybe just a bunch of cattle grazing, and they would look at each other and smile.

Bryson, the hands, even Cook, greeted them with such exuberance that it left no doubt they'd been missed.

Later, sitting on the porch, Bryson smoking his pipe, Mason enjoying the quiet and the warm feeling of family around him, and Laura sitting close enough that he could reach out and touch her, Mason was prompted to think there were few things in life better than what he had right here.

Bryson rocked back, chewed on his pipe a second, then took it from his mouth. "Uh . . ." he mumbled.

"All right, Bryson, spit it out. You've been itching to say something ever since we sat down out here."

"Well, it's like this, Mason. I, we, all of us ranchers appreciate what you're doing for us. Now you've gone and got yourself shot up, and I don't feel like we ought to ask any more of you. You've done enough."

"Aw c'mon, Bryson, the job has to get done; besides, I'm a valley rancher too, so I'm also working in my own interest."

Bryson grunted. "Yeah, but," he stammered, "well, hell, knew you wouldn't quit, but I told 'em I'd bring it up to you."

"Would you get me a cup of coffee, little girl? I want to ask your pa something, sort of—well, you shouldn't listen to what I have to say."

He and Laura stood at the same time. She placed her hand on his arm, squeezed it, turned and went in the house. Mason walked over and stood, spread-legged, in front of Bryson.

"I've got something to ask you. I believe you know enough about me so you can answer, and if the answer is 'no,' I'll understand."

"Boy, ask it. I can't think of anything I'd refuse you. Anything I have is yours for the asking."

"Maybe there's one thing you won't give me, Bryson. It's Laura I'm talking about. I want Laura for my wife. I love her. I would never let harm come to her and I'd care for her so she'd never want for anything." Mason sucked in a deep breath and blew it out. "Well, there it is. I've said it."

Bryson squinted through the semidarkness. "I reckon you know this doesn't surprise me. I've seen it coming a pretty good while. Matter of fact, I was beginning to think I was gonna have to give ya a little push in that direction." He chuckled. "Hell, yes, git married! I been wondering how to keep you around here anyway."

Mason looked up as Laura came back with the coffee. "You can sit here, close to me now. Your pa said he was mighty glad someone came along who'd take you off his hands."

"Hey! Hold up, you'll spill that coffee on me," he said, when Laura threw her arms around his neck.

"Cole Mason, you're not going to make me even a little bit mad with all your teasing. Besides, I know my pa wouldn't give me to just any old cowhand. You ought to feel special."

"Laura, I've felt special ever since you said you loved me." Mason was again serious. "But I'm gonna finish the job I've started. After that we'll have the biggest fandango this country's ever seen." He frowned, scratched his jaw, and grinned. "Just thought of somethin'. We're sure gonna mess up any plans they have for a charivari." He threw back his head and laughed. "They'll never find us in Misty Glen. I'll have you all to myself."

"And, even as much as I'm blushing right now, I'm gonna tell you that's just the way I want it, cowboy."

Not long after finishing his coffee, Mason told Laura and her father good night. As much as he wanted to stay with them, he had things to do that couldn't wait. He left the next morning.

He headed for the back country, and when he had been on the trail a couple of hours, he reined the black to a halt before riding into the open. His gaze picked out every spot that could hide a rifleman, but saw no sign that others were around. He kneed his horse out onto the flats.

Slade had declared open season on him. Since the shootout at the herd, he'd not been to town, but his riders had seen Slade's men riding the open country, always heavily armed. Mason ordered them to avoid a confrontation. They had.

Slade really wanted only one man—Cole Mason. With him dead, any semblance of resistance would fold. A rifle shot from a clump of trees, from behind a boulder, or even tall grass was all it would take. Mason used any cover he could find, causing everything he did to take a lot of time—but it kept him alive.

He wanted to stop by his ranch—he was beginning to think of the Larsen place as his—and pick up Brody and Martinez. They needed supplies. He hadn't stocked up real well since taking over, and Murtry and Barkley might have something to tell him also. A trip to town was necessary.

Mason settled his thoughts on Bart Slade. He was one of those flashy gunfighters who was fool enough to believe no one was faster, and Mason believed Slade's enormous ego would keep him from ordering his men to bushwhack him. Slade would probably want to kill him where all could see it happen.

He reined into a sandy draw, in order to make use of the tree cover there, and turned toward the creek. He glanced at the sun and saw it nearing noon. He was hungry.

Reaching the bank, Mason ground-hitched his horse and gathered wood from an old blowdown that some long ago wind had piled in a clump above the high water line. He started his fire.

He had beans and coffee, and was happy to have that. Finished, he doused the fire, scoured his tin dishes with sand, rinsed them, and headed for the ranch. He still faced a long ride into town.

There was nothing to hold him at the ranch, so he bathed, shaved, and changed clothes. Then he headed for town with Brody and Martinez.

They topped a rise and looked down on the faded, sun-bleached buildings. It was about ten-thirty. The few houses that provided shelter for the town's inhabitants were dark. The golden glow of lanterns reflected against the windows of Red Barkley's saloon and the shoddy little hotel also gave a friendly invitation to those out in the chill night. Mason smiled grimly to himself, thinking how wrong that impression of friendliness could be.

He twisted in his saddle. "I'm going in the front door. I'll give you a couple of minutes to go around and come in the back. All I want you to do is cover my back. Don't do any shooting unless I start the music." He moved off, then turned back. "By the way, Barkley, the bartender, is one of us. Trust him."

They tied their horses to the rail in front of the hotel. Brody and Martinez went down the side of the building toward the back.

Mason held up a minute, then pushed through the bat-wing doors and glanced swiftly around the room. Slade was not there, but Hamilton was. He was playing poker at one of the back tables with six of Slade's men. A couple of them looked up, saw Mason, and started to push back from the table.

"Just stay where you are, hands on the table," Mason said. "Hamilton, if you touch your lapels I'll cut that watch chain in two." He nodded. "I'm talking about the one strung across your vest. Just keep riffling those cards and you might be around to order breakfast."

It didn't take a fool to see they wanted no part of him. They froze. They might not know who he was, or where he came from, but he had acquired a considerable local reputation, and that, apparently, was enough.

"Barkley, give Martinez and Brody back there whatever they want. I'll take a glass of that special bourbon you keep under the bar." He never took his eyes off the Slade men.

"Your boss, I want you to give him a message," he continued, as though discussing what they had had for supper. "He's told me several times that I'm a dead man, which sounds like both a brag and a threat. You tell him for me that I'm still waiting." He sipped his drink, looking over the rim at them. "And he has on several occasions wondered who I am. Well, I think every man should know who kills him, so just tell him, 'Cole sent you.' "

There was no doubt that all in the room had heard of Cole. When his name sounded through the room, every man there pushed his hands toward the center of the table at which he sat, and there was total silence. Mason wondered if they even breathed. He tossed his drink down and said, "Ready when you are, Martinez, Brody." He backed out the door. When they met at the hitch rack, Mason said, "Reckon if we figure to keep our good health, we better ride. We'll stock up on supplies some other day."

"You sure as hell layed it on the line," Brody said when they were on the outskirts of town. "I never knew you to do that before." He sounded puzzled.

"You're right. I never have done it before," Mason admitted, "but I figure it may keep me from getting drygulched. If I have Slade figured right, he'll call off his dogs. His ego won't let him admit that anyone is faster, so he'll tell them to leave me alone . . . that he wants me for himself.

"He may not really want me, but he'll have to put up the front anyway. Hamilton isn't like that. He'll see me dead any way he can make it happen. He's a cold customer, but he's getting mad, and that may be his undoing."

It was nearing daylight when they rode into the ranch yard. They'd been halted once. Tom Etheridge, the man Mason had selected from the M-Bar-N, had the last watch of the night, and he stopped them with a cocked rifle until Mason told him who they were.

They told Etheridge the happenings in town, and by the time they'd finished, it was light enough that Mason told him to come on back to the ranch for breakfast.

After breakfast they lingered at the table, talking cattle, range conditions, and the roundup. There was no question but that the ranchers were going to have to sell off some of their cattle. It was not a question of money, since Mason would cover their mortgages. Now the problem was overgrazing, and winter was almost on them. These were old subjects, and through the months past, they'd just about worn them out.

When the men left the table, each to take care of his tasks for the day, Mason sat with his coffee, thinking. Even though he and his men had stymied Slade's rustling, he was flagrantly at it again.

Mason had never been one to put all of his eggs in one basket, but in this case he thought that might be the best bet. The honest ranchers and their hands would be as vigilant as possible. They would slow Slade's operation, but when the last hand was played, it was going to involve every man in the valley, the honest and the crooked.

Slade would have to make a drive soon for the same reasons the ranchers would have to—overgrazing. Mason knew what he planned for that event, and with his plan they would win or lose.

He would be glad when all men could put their guns aside, but even then, he reflected, there would always be men such as Slade and Hamilton with guns, and for this reason honest men would have them too. He got up to go to bed. A day and night in the saddle was enough. He had his share of the ranch to ride tomorrow and it would be a long day.

He slept through the day, and half the night, then puttered around the kitchen until about four o'clock. It was still dark when he saddled for work.

The black wended his way through a thick stand of aspen. Mason guided him with knee pressure. He ducked his head to avoid a limb. When he straightened, he knew what had been trying to push its way into his thoughts. He smelled smoke. It was just a wisp, but enough that his sharply honed senses caught it.

He dismounted, reached around, and cupped his horse's nostrils, then ground-reined him. No more than a shadow, Mason worked his way through the trees. He had gone perhaps a hundred yards, the smell of smoke getting stronger, when he saw the two men bending over a calf, its feet tied with pigging string.

They were in a small clearing, hidden from the view of all eyes except Mason's. He approached to within ten feet before he made them aware he was there.

"Don't turn around, and don't move." His words froze them as though chiseled from stone. "Now, with one hand, unbuckle your gunbelts. Let them fall and step away from them. If you do other than that, Slade's gonna come up two men short."

Their gunbelts hit the ground and they stepped aside. Mason picked the belted guns up and draped them over his shoulder. "Now turn around."

He watched fear flick across their faces when they saw who had them. He glanced at the calf, the fire, and the running iron lying in the coals. "Well, I reckon I don't have to ask what you're up to," he said. "The only problem I seem to have is what shall I do with you.

"I could hang you, but I don't cotton to that very much, or I could give you back your guns and let you try your luck." He nodded thoughtfully, his lips pursed. "Yep, that seems like a pretty good idea."

"I ain't drawin' agin' you, Cole," the tall cowboy said. "Yeah, we all know who you are. When you sent your message back to the ranch half the crew quit and drifted, most of them real hardcases. I ain't even in their class, let alone yours."

"What about you, you want to try your luck?"

The short, stocky cowboy grimaced. "Hell, Mister Cole, I ain't no gunslinger. I ain't even as fast as Slim here. I got no hankerin' to let you use me for target practice."

Mason shook his head as though with a real problem, then squatted and pulled a straw from a weed growing at his feet.

"Well, that makes my problem worse. I don't know what to do with you two. I could—"

"Mister Cole," Shorty cut in, "I got a idear if you'll listen."

Cole nodded. "I'm listening."

"Well, I may be a lot a things, but one thing I ain't, I ain't no liar. You could let us go, an' I promise we'd slope out of here so fast nobody would know we was ever in these parts."

Cole slanted a look up at Slim. "That go for you too?"

"You bet!" Slim exclaimed. "I'll lead the way."

"First, you run a Circle B on that calf and turn 'im loose."

While they were finishing with the calf and dousing the fire, Mason emptied their guns and belts of shells. He handed them back.

"Don't let the sun set on you in this valley. Move out."

"We gotta get our bedrolls back at the ranch." Slim looked as if he thought he might have said too much.

"Get 'em, and keep moving." As they stepped toward their horses, Mason stopped them. "One other thing, if you've got much 'tween those big ears, you'll think a long time before you slap the wrong brand on another cow." He stared at them a long moment. "Get gone."

Mason watched them clear the trees and, once in the open, spur their horses to a run, certain he'd not see them again. He walked back to the clearing, thinking.

Those two were just run-of-the-mill cowboys, and like most, at some time in their hard lives, they'd swung a wide loop. This break he'd just given them might head them onto a straight trail, and keep them there.

He stopped, looked around, and decided to set up camp. He'd spend the rest of the afternoon scouting for sign of more rustlers, and then bed down.

The load on his shoulders seemed much lighter since he'd learned that a goodly bit of Slade's crew had cut out, but that was typical of the breed.

There were honorable men who acquired a reputation, but they didn't travel in wolf packs like Slade's bunch, and the good ones were generally loners. The kind that cottoned to the likes of Slade would stick until the going got rough, then leave. The only thing that held them was the promise of a share of whatever Slade figured on gaining. Mason was sure Slade would not divvy up in the end.

A hard search didn't turn up evidence that others had been in the area. He made a good fire, and when it had died to a glowing bed of coals, he fixed his supper, ate, and sat back to enjoy his coffee.

Thinking back to his Santa Fe trip, he mulled over the list of forts to which Slade was selling cattle. He'd identified not only the forts, but also the names of the buyers, and he knew they had to be in with Slade.

They were probably paying less than market value for the cattle, turning in a voucher to the Army for much more, and pocketing the difference. He reached over and pulled the coffee pot off the coals, poured himself another cup, and leaned against his saddle.

He figured he'd better write the department of the Army a little letter. See if they'd investigate those buyers and get rid of them before the honest ranchers made a trail drive. Otherwise *they* wouldn't get a fair price. It suddenly occurred to him that he was one of those who would be cheated.

Upon returning to the valley, he had scouted for the most likely route over which to drive cattle to those forts.

There was only one that would take them out without adding at least four days to the drive, and that was through the canyon where he'd tangled with the mountain cat. Mason called it Tomahawk Canyon because it looked as though a giant tomahawk had been used to cleave a gorge through the mountain, its sides vertical, as high as three hundred feet in some places, but never lower than one hundred. It was about fifty yards wide, not a good place to be caught when there were heavy thunderstorms in the mountains, but this time of year it was an ideal pass.

He stood, poured another cup of coffee, then sat and leaned against a sapling, thoughtfully tossing twigs into the fire. He wriggled his hips to settle more comfortably into the soft sand at the base of the tree, then leaned over, and using the sand as a drawing board, sketched the canyon as he remembered it.

Almost straight, it had a slight dogleg to the right about a quarter mile from the exit. He strained hard to remember some of the things he had learned at the Point. He had been a good tactician during the War Between the States. Now he wanted to apply some of those principles to mount an offensive against Slade.

There were several things that would be key factors: He had to set it up so he'd know when Slade started the drive; he would have to get word to the ranchers in time for their men to meet him at the head of the canyon, at least a couple of hours before Slade's point rider got there; and he would then have to give his men their position assignments in time for them to get on station.

Also, he had to have dynamite; he wanted each man to have a couple of sticks. This should be some fight, he thought. He reached down, pulled up his blanket, turned on his side, and went to sleep.

He was in the saddle before daylight, wanting to get to the ranch, tell Martinez and Brody the plan, then head for town. He would take the buckboard and Martinez with him.

With this trip he planned to tie all loose ends together.

Squinting, he looked at the horizon. There was a slight lightening of the night sky. He wondered how many times he'd greeted a new day from the saddle. Early morning was his favorite time of day . . . the quiet, the soft rustle of wings as birds began to stir, the last scampering of night creatures running for their burrows before daylight. Too, the air always seemed purer in the early morning hours.

It was full daylight when he reached the ranch. He told Brody to hold up on sending the men out to their daily chores, he wanted to talk to them, and that he and Martinez would be taking the buckboard into town.

Mason had not eaten before he broke camp, so he ate while telling them of his plan. After laying it out and listening to their remarks, he held up his hands for quiet.

"This will only work if the timing is right. Brody, keep everybody close by. Assign each of them a ranch, or ranches, to contact. Each rancher is to meet me with *all* of their hands, ample ammunition, and rifles.

"I'll set it up in town, such that if any of Slade's people let it slip when they are going to start their drive, Barkley or Murtry will send a rider to let us know.

"Also, just in case we don't get word from town, I want a watch set where they are holding the herd. As soon as they show signs of moving out, whoever is on watch will have to hightail it back here and let us know."

"All right, I've got it," Brody said, "and, uh, you and Martinez be careful."

Mason nodded. "You can bet on it." He headed for the door. "Let's hit it, Martinez, we've got a lot to do." As he went out the door, he muttered, "Sure be nice if, for a change, we didn't have any trouble." He knew that was a foolish wish before the words were out of his mouth.

10

MASON HAD NO need to worry about trouble from Slade's men. Those who were not busy with the herd were lazing around the family room in the ranch house Bart Slade had taken over. He liked to keep his men close by.

Slade would not admit it, even to himself, but he was afraid for the first time in his life. He'd heard most of the stories told of Cole. His prowess with handgun, rifle, Bowie knife, throwing knife—and his fists—was legend.

Slade thought about his own reputation, and knew that it had been made by shooting two-bit gun tramps, and picking fights with young cowboys, most of whom were just in town for a Saturday night and had had too much to drink. Even the best of them had no claim to being good with a gun.

This was the first time his speed and accuracy would be tested—and he was afraid.

He walked from room to room, carrying a full glass of whisky. He'd stop, take a swallow, curse, and then continue his pacing, talking to himself. "The damned ranchers with that meddling son of a bitch's help could wipe out everything I've done here. Half my crew . . . *half* of them, the yellow bastards, quit just hearing his name.

"I don't have the odds on my side anymore, and those that are still here will more than likely cut out as soon as the ranchers put up a fight of any kind."

He stopped, drank the rest of his drink, and threw the glass at the window closest to him. He was going to have to fight for everything he got from now on, and he didn't like the idea.

Slade looked around the room, searching for Cash Willough-by, his trail boss. Willoughby was out of Texas, from over Fort Worth way. Luke Short, who owned the White Elephant

Saloon, had caught him pulling an ace off the bottom of the deck and told him to leave town or make use of the .44 he was packing. Willoughby was no coward, but he knew he couldn't beat Short, so he left.

"Willoughby, what's the count out at the herd?"

"Upward of four thousand. Still got about five hundred to go," Willoughby said. "The boys are bringing in forty to fifty head a day."

He looked up at Slade from where he was sitting. "I'll tell you somethin' else, Slade, we better forget the rest a them cows and get on the trail with what we got. Cole, and those ranchers, ain't gonna stand for much more out a us. They—"

"To hell with what you think. I ain't takin' nothin' off of Cole—or the ranchers. They're all gutless, except Cole, and he's just one man. We got an order for forty-five hundred head, and that's what we're delivering."

Willoughby shrugged, indolently. "All right, all right," he answered, then raised his eyebrows and grinned. "It's your funeral."

Slade felt his face drain of color, anger and fear clouding his thinking. He squared off, facing Willoughby, fingertips brushing the walnut grip of his .44. "Don't you ever talk that way to me. You want to try to make it my funeral?"

"Save it for Cole, Slade. You're gonna need all of us, so cool down." Willoughby leaned, picked up his drink from the floor beside his chair, took a swallow, and looked coolly over the rim at Slade.

Slade stared at him a second, then turned and started pacing again. He was going to make the drive, and he was going to deliver forty-five hundred head, not one damn cow less.

He'd take on Mister Gunslinger Cole after delivering the herd. Slade frowned and slowed his pacing. He'd wait for Cole to go to town. He never took but one or two of his hands with him, and that would not be enough to stand up to the Slade crew.

"I'll split the crew, and have half come in from each end of town." He grinned slyly, thinking he'd probably not even have to make a move for his gun if one of the boys got excited and shot Cole from behind. Yeah, he thought, and I'll even put on a show for missing the chance to get him myself. The anger, frustration, and fear seemed suddenly to leave him.

He walked over, filled his glass, and stopped in front of a crewman slouched down in a chair in front of the fireplace. "Get out of that chair," he said.

The young cowboy jumped to his feet. "Yes, sir!" he replied. He walked across the room and sat on the floor.

Slade sat down, still thinking about how he could handle Cole when the time came. He wanted to meet him out on the street, where he'd not have a chance to get his back to a wall. On the street Slade figured to use his full crew, any one of whom could fire at Cole—from in front, or behind.

Bart Slade didn't give a damn how they got him, or from where. He just wanted him cut down like a poleaxed steer, and if he timed *his* draw right, he'd take credit for killing the mighty Cole. If he played it close, his name would be known all over the country.

Had he known what Mason was up to at that very minute, he'd have started pacing again, because only fifteen miles away, Mason and Martinez were carefully storing the last of several boxes of dynamite in the wagon.

"Señor, I theenk we could blow up evertheeng west of Tejas." Martinez's teeth gleamed at Cole. "What you theenk, amigo?"

Mason laughed. "I think you are right, well maybe not *everything* west of Texas, but almost." He gingerly placed the last box on the wagon bed, straightened, and jumped to the ground, "Let's get a beer. I'm hotter'n a two-dollar pistol."

"I theenk maybe you forget those words." Martinez headed toward the saloon. It was obvious he was a thirsty man.

Mason glanced around the big room and saw that they had the place to themselves. Barkley drew two beers, being careful to leave only a small head on each, then reached under the counter and pulled out a sawed-off twelve-gauge shotgun.

"Loaded with buckshot," he said, patting the stock. "Murtry's got one just like it and, Mason, most of the town's people will back you. They ain't fightin' men, but this here Hamilton-Slade thing's put a burr under their saddles." He winked at Mason. "They ain't gonna let nobody get at your back."

"Hmmm, looks like the odds have tilted in our favor for a change." Mason slapped Martinez on the shoulder. "Hey, amigo, this calls for another beer. You too, Barkley. I'm buying."

Before leaving town, Mason walked the length of Main Street. It was only a couple of hundred yards long, with false-fronted buildings on both sides. He looked for positions from which a rifleman could fire with relative safety and still cover most of the street.

He snorted in disgust, thinking that anybody behind those old weathered boards would get slivers blown clean through him. I'd rather take my chances down in the middle of the street he thought. He spun on his heel and headed back to the wagon, where he saw Martinez slouched on the seat.

The wagon had been left in front of the general store. Mason motioned for Martinez to come on down with the wagon. It was time they left town, before trouble caught up with them.

They'd not driven but a couple of miles when Mason motioned Martinez to stop the wagon.

"You ready to take an extra day's ride?"

Martinez shrugged. "You're the boss. Where you take us now, señor?"

"Well, we aren't over seven or eight miles from Tomahawk Canyon. We could save a lot of time by taking this dynamite up there and caching it now rather than hauling it all the way to the ranch and then back to the canyon."

He flicked a thumb toward the wagon bed. "We have a tarp to put over it, and then, with a whole hell of a lot of care, we'll cover it all with rocks or maybe find a blowdown. We'll put it up on the rim. Slade's people will have no reason to be there, so there isn't much chance anyone will find it."

Martinez squinted thoughtfully. "I theenk maybe ees good idea, but after we hide eet, I theenk we must come back almost to town, so we don't come close to Slade's place, sí?"

Mason raised his eyebrows and smiled. "Sí, amigo, we'll do it that way."

A gentle tug on the reins, and the team pulled off the trail, headed for the canyon. Mason slouched in the seat, eyelids almost closed, and admired Martinez's deft handling of the horses. When it seemed that they were sure to roll over a rock, Martinez managed somehow to make the wheels miss it.

"Gotta wonder, amigo, if you drive this well all the time—or could the load we're carrying have anything to do with it?"

Martinez flashed him a smile. "Señor, why do you theenk I get hold of the reins so queek when we get in the wagon.

Oh, sí, I trust you—but not so much as me." He smiled again.
"But, señor, when we get theez dynamite unloaded, I'll let you
drive all the way home."

"Yeah, while you crawl in the back and sleep I'll bet.
But, being a good friend, I reckon you got a deal. I'll drive
home."

When they reached the rim of the canyon, Mason told
Martinez to drive on about a quarter of a mile. He thought
he saw a blowdown that looked to be a good place to hide
the dynamite. It turned out he was right.

Very gently, they stacked the boxes next to the blowdown,
covered them with the tarp, and then pulled limbs and brush
over the pile. They stood back and looked at the hiding place,
then walked to a different viewpoint and looked again. Assured
that unless someone knew it was there, it would not be found,
they climbed back in the wagon and headed for home. Mason
drove only partway. Martinez said Mason hit too many bumps,
and he again took the reins.

He parked by the kitchen door in order to unload the supplies. He and Mason had hardly gotten their feet on the ground
when Brody rounded the corner of the house.

"Where the hell y'all been?" he yelled. "We was about ready
to ride out lookin' for ya."

"Get the boys and let's get the wagon unloaded, then I'll
tell all of you what we been doing," Mason said, and at the
same time he was flooded with warm feeling for his men.
They cared about each other as only those who have worked
and fought together can feel.

"Any grub left?" Martinez asked. "I could eat the south
end of a northbound burro, and I theenk Señor Mason ees
a leetle hongry too. He chewed two feet off the reins on the
way in. We ain't et since yesterday morning—two days, no
grub."

They joked, laughed, and poked fun at each other while
unloading the provisions. The rest of the crew joined the work
party, so they made short work of it.

"Hey, I see ya got some dried apples," Britt Henry of the
Bar H, said. "We gonna have some apple pie?"

Mason nodded. "Yep."

"Who's gonna cook it?" Jack Rains asked. "They ain't
nobody round this bunch can cook worth a damn."

"Hey, men, sounds like we got us a volunteer to do all the cooking," Tim Matlock said.

Rains turned red. "Aw, I ain't complainin'." He grinned sheepishly. "Besides, y'all wouldn't eat my cookin' anyway."

"I don't know who cooked supper tonight," Mason said, pushing back from the table, "but that meal was plumb fit to eat." He patted his stomach, a satisfied fullness pervading him.

"C'mon in the front room, and Martinez and I'll tell you why we were so late getting back." He turned to Britt. "As for the apples, I thought I'd ride over tomorrow and see if Miss Laura will come over and fix us some pies. Sure not gonna chance any of you messing em up." Then, feeling sheepish, he smiled. "I reckon I'll tell y'all now. As soon as we finish this thing with Slade, Miss Laura and I are going to get married."

He felt Martinez's arm go around his shoulders. "Hey, amigos, he tells us the beeg secret, eh?" Martinez looked at Mason straight on. "Boss, ever seence you get all shot up an' that leetle girl seet by your bed the whole time, we all know. We just don't know when."

Mason and his men sat in the front room talking well into the night. He sketched exactly where the dynamite was cached, so that any of them would know where it was and what to do with it when the time came. Finally he looked around the room at each of them.

"Those of you who don't want apple pie tomorrow can sit here and talk the rest of the night, but I'm going to bed." He looked around. He was talking to an empty room.

Mason seldom smoked, but tonight he plucked a cigar out of the humidor and walked outside. At the corral, he climbed up, sat on the top rail, and breathed deeply. These scents, he thought, we seldom notice them, but if they weren't here, we'd feel like we were in a foreign world.

A faint suggestion of dust, mingled with a trace of wood smoke, frost-killed grass, and the pungent scent of horse droppings, clung to the crisp fall night.

Mason sighed. This was where he belonged, he thought. He, his woman, his men—and their womenfolk when they were ready for it. The shrill song of crickets, the strident call of locusts—all of the natural night sounds caused him to relax.

He was so attuned to his surroundings that the slightest sound, or lack of it, focused all of his senses, but tonight was one in which he sensed that all was right. He finished his cigar and went in to bed.

The next morning Mason started to saddle the big black, but then decided to let him rest. The line-back dun was almost as good, especially for staying power. He wasn't quite as fast as the black, but he could run all day.

He rode out of the stable, to find that it had started to drizzle, and almost turned back into the warmth and dryness.

He shook out his slicker, shrugged into it, and made sure his moccasins were in his bedroll. He liked wearing them of an evening when sitting in front of a good fire. Assured that everything was to his liking, he pulled his hat down on his forehead and rode out, head bent into the steady, penetrating rain.

Day broke gray and gloomy. He'd been on the trail almost two hours. It would take another three, maybe four hours to reach Bryson's place, and the way the sky looked, he'd be wet all the way.

The thought of the cheery Circle B kitchen and a hot cup of coffee was cause enough for him to kick the dun into a faster gait.

He forded the creek, which was almost bank full, an indication that the rain was heavy in the higher elevations. Climbing the bank on the other side, he saw them—fresh tracks.

His first thought was that Slade had picked a perfect day to bedevil the ranchers. Everyone would be indoors unless there was something that just had to be done, and there were few things couldn't be put off another day.

He looked closer at the tracks. He reined in, dismounted, and squatted to study them a few moments. Very little water had seeped into them, so they were clear, well-defined prints. The horses that had made them were only a few minutes ahead of him. There were ten horses in the bunch, all carrying a rider, and there was not a shod horse among them.

Not Slade this time, Mason thought, Indians, probably Apache. He felt a chill run up his spine, knowing they were no more than a few minutes ahead. They were probably intent on stealing horses, but if they were wearing paint, hell was riding the range.

He ground-reined the dun and crawled to the lip of the creek bank. He slowly raised his head and peered over—not an Indian in sight.

Mason slid down and took the dun's reins, then thought to leave him and wear moccasins to follow the raiding party. He discarded that idea as soon as it surfaced, not wanting to be afoot with no way to make a run for it.

There was not a meaner or more dangerous fighting man anywhere than an Apache warrior. Mason understood them, respected them, but wasn't fool enough to tangle with ten of them. He'd been initiated as a Sioux warrior and was blood brother to Fighting Wolf, a war chief without peer.

He had witnessed men die, slowly, painfully, at the hands of the Apaches, who never considered that what they did might be cruel; the word was not part of their language. It was their way of life and Mason understood that. This reinforced his determination not to provide them with that kind of entertainment.

He mounted the dun. As soon as he had the advantage of this elevation, he saw them cresting a knoll about three hundred yards ahead. One of them looked back toward Mason.

He froze, knowing that if he did not move he would be hard to see against the tangle of trees that huddled along the creek bank. The brave turned his head back to the others. Mason slid from the saddle. He'd lead the horse in order to decrease the chance of becoming skylined.

The Apache route was directly toward the Circle B. Even if they were a war party, and he thought they were, Mason knew they would not just ride in on the ranch. They'd stop, send out a scouting party, and then talk when the scouts returned. But whatever they were up to, Mason knew he'd better find out what it was and warn Bryson.

The Apaches dipped into a swale, and Mason knew even the brownish gray of the trees behind him would do little to camouflage him. They'd be looking up toward the lighter sky, and he'd show plainly against it. As much as he hated it, he'd have to leave his horse.

He backtracked to the creek, losing time, but thinking it better to lose a little now than a lot later staked out on an anthill or bed of coals in order to furnish the Apaches an evening's fun.

He took moccasins from his saddlebags, stripped the gear off the dun, and slapped him gently on the rump, hoping he would return to the ranch for shelter and a belly full of grain. He was thankful now he'd pampered this horse right along with the black.

He wrapped his boots and tack in the saddle blanket and slicker, then cached them under a washout, behind a cluster of roots. Mason shivered as the rain pelted his now unprotected back. As much as he hated the idea of not wearing it, that slicker would be too visible and noisy, so he left it.

Afoot and bent over to take advantage of the cover the tall grass afforded, Mason was wary of closing on the raiders too fast. They were in no hurry, and he saw that they were taking care not to stumble upon a lone rider. Surprise was their strength.

When he approached the swale into which he'd seen them disappear, he dropped to his stomach and, cradling his Winchester in the crooks of his elbows, slithered toward where he'd last seen them. To his relief he discovered that they had ridden on. If he had them figured right, they would get closer to the ranch before stopping.

Inching to his knees, Mason peered across the limp sea of grass and saw them, still about a quarter of a mile ahead, in single file, slouched on the backs of their wet, bedraggled ponies.

Each time one of them dropped back to scout their rear, Mason hit the ground, and stayed there until the scout turned back to join the others.

Several sodden, uneventful miles passed under his squishing moccasins, and he was thankful every step he took that the wind was in his face; their ponies had no chance of picking up his scent.

A stream lay ahead, and by Mason's reckoning it was only a little less than two miles to the Circle B. He'd thought all along that Bryson's place would be their destination. Now he was sure.

He had to get there ahead of them. He had to warn Bryson. He came up with several ideas as to how to do it, but discarded each. They were either too time-consuming, impractical, or sure death—for him.

Suddenly, the Apaches disappeared. He'd lost sight of them. Then he remembered the stream. If he had them figured right, they would stop in the trees that bordered it, make a small fire, and eat.

This extra time would allow him to circle around and make a run for the ranch. He hated to get closer to them, but he had to know if he was right, that they were really in those trees bordering the stream. The only way to know was to look.

Even with the bone-chilling cold of the rain, he was sweating, and a hard, roiling knot had settled in the pit of his stomach. He could think of a lot of things he'd rather do than try to sneak up on a band of Apaches.

He dropped to his stomach and dragged himself toward a point upstream of where they'd disappeared. It was slow going trying to keep his rifle clear of the mud and work his way through the matted grass that seemed determined to pull it out of the crook of his elbows.

He'd been close enough several times to see the arms they carried. Every member of the band was armed with an excellent piece—a Winchester .44–.40 rifle. Hot bile boiled into Mason's throat. What breed of snake sold rifles to the Apaches, knowing they'd be used against whites?

He estimated he was getting close to the stream and slowed his pace, being extra careful to make no noise. He parted the grass in front of him and discovered that the creek bank dropped off right under where his hands held the grass apart—and he was eyeball to eyeball with one of the Apaches.

Without thinking, Mason reached out with both hands and circled the Indian's neck. The Indian had no chance to give warning. Eyes bulging, he tried to grab for his knife.

Every muscle in his shoulders and forearms straining, seeming about to tear out of his skin, Mason pushed up hard with his thumbs under the warrior's chin, his fingers locked behind the Apache's neck.

Veins stood out as large as fingers in the Indian's forehead and temples, resisting Mason's effort to snap his neck. Mason knew his thumbs would not withstand the pressure much longer. Mustering every ounce of strength in his chest, arms, and shoulders, he jerked upward toward himself. He felt, and heard, a grinding snap under his fingers.

The Apache went limp. Still clinging to the oddly twisted head and neck, and inching back from the bank, Mason dragged the lifeless Indian up and over the lip. There was no question now. He had to get out of here, for it would not be long before the war party missed their companion.

He looked down at the brown face, painted for war, eyes staring at nothing. The warrior still clutched his rifle. Mason took the rifle and carefully packed mud down the barrel, then left it beside its owner.

Slithering backward, he circled the spot in which he knew the war party was nooning. He stopped and sniffed, catching a faint whiff of wood smoke. Once again he was thankful for being downwind. They would be there awhile, at least until they missed their companion and went to look for him. Then all hell would break loose.

Mason stopped, looked back, and judged he'd circled far enough to avoid getting upwind, from where the horses could pick up his scent.

Standing, he headed for the ranch in a running, bent-over gait. He had put about a mile behind him when he straightened and lengthened his stride.

He breathed deeply for the first time and felt the life-giving air go deeply into his lungs. When he bent, air failed to reach the depths of his lungs, and he needed every bit of breath possible now—if he was to stay ahead of the Indians.

Another quarter mile and he heard their shrill cries of anger. A glance over his shoulder told him he'd been seen.

They were mounted and coming at a belly-to-the-ground run. He quickened and lengthened his stride. Pacing himself now would only get him caught. If he couldn't get to the ranch before giving out, the Apaches would make sport of him by their fire when night fell.

Where the grass had been an ally when Mason needed cover, it now became an enemy. He had to lift his legs so his feet would clear it and not cause him to trip. He could run all day in the forest or short grass prairie, but this unnatural stride he was forced into was sucking energy already strained to the limit.

He crested the hill above the ranch and saw the house and outbuildings show ghostly through the rain. Smoke curled lazily from the chimney, then bent to lie close to the ground, as though trying to escape the bleak atmosphere it was being exiled to.

Mason's legs were leaden; it seemed each had an anvil tied to it. Breath forced into his lungs caused his side to burn, feeling as though a hot knife pierced it every time his lungs expanded.

God, he thought, please let me get to one of the outbuildings, where I'll have cover. Once he started firing, those in the ranch and bunkhouse would hear the shots and be warned. Then whatever happened, he'd have done what he had to.

The Apaches were close now, and were throwing shots, some close enough he heard them whine past. About two hundred yards now. If I don't take a slug in my legs or head, I'll get there, he thought detachedly, as though he were standing aside and watching the pursuit of another person.

Now! He was close enough. He pulled his rifle up in front of his chest and fired three shots into the air as fast as he could lever shells into the chamber.

There was only a wagon between him and the barn door. He jumped the tongue, fell, and rolled through the door, coming to rest on his stomach, facing the fast-approaching Apaches.

He continued firing. They were only a couple of hundred yards out—a good range for scoring sure hits. One of the braves threw his arms wide and fell from his pony. The rest scattered.

Mason reloaded, aware his shots had been heard. Rifles were talking from every window.

The raiding party made one circle of the house, then withdrew out of rifle range. They gathered around their leader, who circled his hand above his head and dropped it to point away from the ranch, obviously motioning them to leave.

With the rain, they had probably figured to catch everyone inside, launch a surprise attack, loot, burn, and leave. Mason had a hunch, based on the luck they'd had here, that they'd head for a different area.

He pulled his knees under him and stood. His eyes wouldn't focus and he felt weak. Then he saw the blood dripping from his hand and realized that at least one of the Apache's bullets had done more than whine past. He stepped toward the ranch house. Laura, Bryson, and the hands met him halfway.

"Get back in the house out of this rain," he shouted.

"Hot damn! I knew it was you. Ain't nobody else around can raise so much hell all to onct," one of the young hands yelled, slapped his thigh, then looked sheepishly at Laura. "Sorry, Miss Laura, reckon I forgot m'self."

"Well, hot dammit, reckon you're right," Laura mimicked, catching them all by surprise.

Laughter swelled around Mason as Laura took his arm. He winced. She released his arm and stood back to look at him.

"You're hit. Bad?"

He shook his head. "A crease. The blood makes it look worse than it is. C'mon, let's get inside outta the rain."

Tilghman posted one of the hands to keep watch. The rest of them gathered around Mason in front of the fire while Laura dressed the crease he'd gotten across his shoulder.

"There, that'll take care of it," Laura said as she tied the last edge of the bandage down.

"You know, lad," Bryson squinted at Mason through a cloud of smoke from his pipe, "I ain't never seen a man that beds down with trouble the way you do. I ain't figured out whether you look for it, or it just stays perched on your shoulder waitin' fer a place to happen."

"Well, I'll tell you honest, Bryson, I sure don't look for it. If it's there, I reckon I don't try to walk around it. Maybe that's my answer—I just need to try harder to avoid it. Seems like . . ."

"Humph!" Laura gave a very unladylike snort. "That'll be a sight to see, Cole Mason walking around trouble. Humph!" she repeated. "When I was nursing you back from the edge of death, over at the Snake, Sisson and I counted twenty-three knife and bullet scars on you, and that was just where I could see. You wait'll we're married; I'll put a stop to all that fighting. I'll be keeping a close eye on you my wild and woolly friend."

"I don't reckon you'll have any trouble doing that," Mason said, looking into her eyes. "I'm figuring to stay right close to you, till you run me off."

Laura flushed to the roots of her auburn hair.

Seeing she was embarrassed, Mason changed the subject. "I s'pose y'all want to know why I rode all this way in the rain. Well, the reason is, the boys have worked up a terrible, consuming hunger for some of your apple pie, Laura, and rather than have them all ride over here, I thought maybe I could talk you into coming over to my place." He looked at Bryson. "She'll be safe, Bryson. I'll take good care of her."

"I know you will, lad. I don't worry when she's with you." His face crinkled into a grin. "Now that you're here, you can get your fill of her pie before the boys cut you out." He turned to Tilghman. "Reckon the excitement's over, but maybe it would be a good idea to keep a watch posted tonight. Don't b'lieve they'll be back, but might as well play it safe."

Tilghman stood and signaled the hands it was time to go. When they'd closed the door behind them, Laura went to the kitchen to get Mason's pie and coffee. When she returned, he was slouched down in his chair, asleep. She smiled and took the pie back to the kitchen.

11

THEY HAD BEEN riding an hour when the sun lifted above the mountains. Mason rode a borrowed horse, bareback, wanting to pick up his own rig and not wanting to bother carrying the extra saddle. Bareback caused him no trouble. When living with the Sioux, he'd never used a saddle. He looked at Laura and smiled. Her green eyes lit up. It was a beautiful day.

Even though the Apaches had probably gone home, there was still Slade and his men to worry about, so they rode the low places, warily approaching each ravine, streambed, or clump of trees.

The streams, usually placid, were roiling, muddy serpents, crashing over rocks, angrily dragging old tree skeletons in their grasp. Mason was glad now for the time he'd spent scouting the valley, and was rewarded for it again. He knew where the fords were, and they made it safely across them, although wet to their boot tops.

He retrieved his gear from its cache, saddled, and rode on.

When they'd ridden an hour since picking up his rig, he suddenly reined his horse to a halt.

"Rider comin' hell for leather," he said. "Keep me between you and him." The rider closed on them, and Mason recognized him.

"It's all right, Laura. It's Rod Juarez, one of my men, but judging by the way he's riding, something's bad wrong."

They waited. Juarez was almost on top of them when he pulled his horse in to a sliding halt.

"Boss," he shouted, "old Sam Sisson's been shot." Then, apparently remembering his manners, he tipped his hat to Laura. "Mornin', Miss Laura."

126

"Where, when, why?" Mason shot questions at him faster than he could answer. Mason reined his horse around and dug in his spurs. "C'mon, tell me about it on the way." He felt as if someone had hit him in the gut; his mind churned with thoughts of Sisson. He'd grown to love the lonely old man.

Whoever had done it would pay, he'd see to that, but why, why would anyone want to hurt Sisson? He never bothered anybody—just worked like hell taking care of the ranch he loved. Sisson wasn't an outgoing man, which caused many to think of him as crotchety, but Mason and Laura had learned better. Sisson had let down his defenses with them and was their friend.

While riding, Mason learned that when Juarez had told them Sisson had been shot, he'd said all he knew of the incident.

"Laura, you come with me. We'll cut cross-range to the Snake." He twisted in his saddle to face Juarez. "Go back to the ranch and tell the boys where we are, and we'll get to the ranch when they see us, then you come on over to the Snake. It's not going to help any to kill your mount, cowboy." With that, he reined his horse around, and he and Laura rode for the Snake.

When they drew rein in front of Sisson's house, there were several horses tied to the rail. Laura dismounted on the run, without waiting for Mason to help her down. He tied both horses and followed her.

Sisson was in bed, his head swathed in bandages, his face tinged with the pallor of death. Mason saw that what could be done had been done. He turned to Sisson's foreman, Nolen Chisolm.

"What happened, Chisolm?"

"Damned if I know, Mason. Me an' the boys rode in for supper and found him crumpled up on the porch, his gun still in its holster. Reckon he must've knowed whoever done it. Ain't no doubt in my mind he took a gunshot to the head— a deep crease. Ain't no way he could've fell an' done it."

"I think you're right." Mason glanced at Laura and saw she was checking Sisson's pulse. "How's he seem to be, Laura?"

She gently placed Sisson's arm back under the blanket. "His pulse is strong, but sort of irregular. I think about all we can do is sit and wait."

"You go on and get some supper. I'll stay here with him."

She started to protest, but Mason cut her off. "You've had a hard day. I'll eat when you're through."

He motioned Chisolm closer. "Take the men and make sure they get fed; then you all get some sleep. I'll give a yell if anything changes here."

After they'd eaten, he and Laura settled in for the long night's vigil. Mason turned the lantern down to a soft, shimmering glow, then looked over at Laura. She was asleep. He found a blanket and tucked it around her, then touched the backs of his fingers to her cheek. She snuggled farther into the blanket and smiled, never waking.

Mason checked Sisson every half hour or so, to see if his pulse rate had changed, or if he'd gotten feverish, but the old man seemed to be the same as when he and Laura arrived.

The new day awakened. A rooster crowed, a burro brayed, a mockingbird trilled its song to herald the day's coming, but Sisson didn't stir. Mason placed his fingers on the old man's neck, over the large artery that pulsed there; it was strong and regular. He sighed. "Old-timer, you're gonna make it."

Mason slouched in his chair and dozed. Between sleep and wakefulness he became aware of the mingled smells of morning. The aroma of brewing coffee mixed with the appetite-stirring smell of frying bacon and drew his attention to his stomach; the feeling was like a sharp rebuke for having been forgotten.

He looked at Sisson and whispered, "I'm gonna get something to eat before there's two of us in that bed, old-timer." A glance at Laura showed she still slept. He slipped out of the room.

It had been Sisson's way to eat with the crew. This served a dual purpose; it gave him company, and the chance to discuss the day's chores.

Mason watched the members of the crew straggle in, or out. They would look stone-faced at Sisson's chair, and then look away. Mason tried to reassure each of them that he thought Sisson would make it, but his words seemed to fall on deaf ears.

They were for the most part old-timers used to violence, but somehow, all seemed to have thought Sisson indestructible, that he would always be there, and now he was seriously wounded. It took some of the starch out of them.

Mason finished breakfast, poured a cup of coffee for Laura, and took it to the room with him.

Upon entering the room, he glanced at Sisson, then at Laura, and thought how beautiful she was, her hair tousled and curly about her face, long lashes resting on her cheeks. He hated to wake her, but walked over and touched her shoulder. Her eyelids parted, heavy with sleep, then she sat up, quickly, and looked at Sisson.

"He's all right, Laura. I believe he's gonna make it. His pulse is strong and regular, but he's still unconscious." He handed her the coffee. "Here, this will wake you up."

"You let me sleep all night. Why didn't you wake me?"

"Because you were a very tired girl, and you needed rest more than me. I think now that you're awake *I'll* take a little siesta."

He started toward the big leather-bound chair in which he had spent the night, then turned back to Laura. "Laura, ask Chisolm to send one of his hands over to the Circle B. Have him tell your pa where we are, and that we'll be staying until Sisson's better." He walked to the chair, sat down, and was instantly asleep.

The shadows were long into the afternoon when Mason stirred and opened his eyes. Laura sat by the bed, holding Sisson's gnarled hand in hers. She talked to him as though he were awake, encouraging him to fight, to climb out of the deep well of darkness that engulfed him. Mason knew then how she'd fought for him when *he'd* been so sorely wounded.

He pushed up out of the chair, walked over, and put his hand on her shoulder, then leaned over and kissed her cheek. She looked up, and he saw dark circles under her eyes.

"He stirred twice, and each time he tried to say something, but just mumbled. I couldn't understand what he tried to say."

"That's all right. We don't want him trying to talk until he's stronger." Mason looked at the rugged, kind old man lying there. "I just want to find out who did this." He left the room, wanting to wash his face and try to wake up.

On the way out he went by the stove and gathered some of the white ash into his palm to use as pumice to brush his teeth. On the way to the pump, he broke a twig from the privet hedge and chewed the end into a makeshift toothbrush.

After brushing his teeth, he rubbed his palm across his cheek and decided to shave and bathe. Unlike many, if there was enough water, Mason bathed every day.

Clean from the skin out, he slipped quietly back into Sisson's room. "How is he?"

"I think he's trying to wake up," Laura replied, then looked directly at him. "You shaved, and bathed. You smell nice."

Sisson groaned. They turned to look at him. His eyes opened a slit, then closed, then opened again, wider. He stared blankly at the ceiling. "Wh-what happened?"

"Don't try to talk, Sisson. You're gonna be all right now, so take it easy."

"Should've known y'all would be here if I needed you." Sisson smiled weakly, then licked his lips. "Water . . . dry as cotton."

Laura held a dipper to his mouth. After a few swallows he nodded slightly and closed his eyes.

"He's asleep now, not unconscious. He'll make it," Mason said.

Mason spread his blanket on the floor by Sisson's bed. He insisted that Laura go to bed and get a good night's sleep.

"Where the hell is everybody?" he heard Sisson growl later. "I'm hungrier'n a b'ar after winter sleep."

Mason stretched and stood to look down at the old-timer. The morning sun streaming through the window showed him that Sisson's eyes were clear.

"Humph! Here we are worrying about you and all you can think of is your stomach. How're you feeling, old friend?"

" 'Ceptin fer a helluva headache, I'm all right." He looked past Mason. "Where's Laura?"

"Probably still asleep. I'll go round us up some breakfast. You just stay put till I get back."

"Your breakfast is on the kitchen table," Laura said from the door. "I have Sam's here." She walked to the bed and smiled down at Sisson. "You gave us a scare. Do you feel like talking about it?"

"Let Mason go eat. I'll tell you both about it after I surround that breakfast you brought me."

When Mason had eaten and come back into the room, he pulled a chair up close for Laura, then sat on the edge of the bed. Sisson looked at them, grunted, and said, "Now I'll tell ya what happened.

"The crew had all left to attend their chores, and Chisolm had taken a few of them down to mend fence when Neal Hamilton rode in. Wondered what he was doin' on the Snake. I never borrowed money from nobody. Don't intend to.

"Well, anyhow, first off he tried to loan me money for improvements, said he'd looked over the place when riding in, and the improvements I needed were gonna be costly.

"I told him flatly I didn't need his damned money; then he tried to buy me out. We'd both got ourselves a little huffy by then. I ordered him to get the hell off my ranch and stay off. It was then I started to slap my leg, you know, like you seen me do a hundred times when I say something I really mean.

"Well, Hamilton musta thought I was goin' fer my gun, 'cause next thing I knew was Hamilton lookin' meaner'n hell and firin' at me. That's the last thing I remember."

Mason nodded. "He probably thought he'd killed you. He couldn't have known his slug traveled around your skull and under your scalp without puttin' a hole through that hard head of yours. You're lucky, Sisson. The way I figure it, Neal Hamilton is more dangerous than Bart Slade and his men combined." Reaching behind his head, Mason rubbed his neck, trying to work the stiffness from it, then looked at Sisson.

"You know, at first his attack on you didn't make sense, but the more I think about it, it does. Look at it this way: The Snake is adjacent to his ranch; with it, he'd not have to fence, and it would more than double the size of his place. It'd give him borders on two more ranches . . . make it easier to strip them of cattle."

Mason paced across the room and back. "I wish we had some law in this valley. We don't, so I reckon it's up to us to clean it up. The day's coming, though, when there *will* be law, and we'll all be able to hang up our guns."

They stayed with Sisson three more days. By then he was up and around. Before leaving, Mason told Chisolm to be sure Sisson took it easy. "If he doesn't, you come get me, Chisolm, and I'll put him back to bed."

"Like hell," Mason heard Sisson growl as he and Laura rode off.

Laura worked all day baking pies for Mason's crew. When she had the last four in the oven, she poured herself and Mason cups of coffee, sighed, and sat down at the kitchen table, mopping her brow.

"Do you realize you've been underfoot all day?" she asked. "And you've eaten five pieces of pie. If I don't want a fat husband, I'll have to schedule bake days few and far between."

"Aw, you wouldn't do that, would you? I'd promise to stay out of the way."

Laura burst out laughing. "Oh, Cole, sometimes you're like a little boy, and I love you for it. Of course, I wouldn't do that."

She laughed again, then looked toward the oven. "They'll be ready by supper time, and in spite of you, there will be plenty for everyone. You see, every time you ate a slice, I just increased my recipe by another pie." She laughed again. Her laugh was like music to Mason, the happiest he'd ever heard.

"We better get to bed early. I want to get you back to the Circle B because if I—"

"Oh! I work all day baking for you and your crew, and once it's done, you want to get rid of me."

"Oh, c'mon, Laura," Mason protested, not realizing she was again teasing him. "It's just that if Slade starts to move the herd, we're going to have to act fast, and I don't want you riding around the range alone. I want you at home, safe."

Because of the Sisson shooting, Mason used extra care while escorting Laura back to the Circle B. The route he picked was faster, yet afforded good cover. He studied the skyline constantly as they rode.

It was as though they were all alone in the world until they rode around the shoulder of the hill that overlooked the ranch. Mason's gaze searched all of the places that might hide a man, and saw no one between them and the ranch. They were home safe.

Immediately surrounded by Bryson and his crew, Mason told them what had happened on the Snake, but didn't add his suspicions to the account. Now was the time for hard fact to be followed up with action. He wanted to think, and the best place for him to do that was under the stars. He told them good-bye and set out for his ranch. He'd make camp when about halfway home.

The stars seemed close enough to touch. The night sounds, the velvet dark, the fresh smell of prairie grass, and the taste of wood smoke gave Mason a sense of oneness with the universe.

He puzzled over the connection between Bart Slade and Neal Hamilton. With no proof they were working together, all of the evidence still pointed in that direction. Even without facts, his gut convinced him they were partners.

Plan as he would, the solution always came down to guns. He was in a box canyon, with only one way out.

He stood, walked over, and kicked dirt on the few coals remaining from his fire. He wondered how many lives would be snuffed out as easily as the fire. He stared at the smoldering coals, then said, "Que sera, sera."

When he awoke, he lay motionless, his senses becoming attuned to all around him. Satisfied he was alone, he rolled out of his blanket. His bedding was damp from heavy dew; Mason would try to remember to dry it when he got home. He saddled the dun, tied his blanket roll behind the saddle, and mounted. While riding, he chewed a strip of jerky, knowing there'd be a good meal when he got to the ranch. Suddenly, he reined his horse to a halt and decided to check one more time on what was happening in town. He kneed the dun off the trail and headed cross-country, it would be shorter than cutting back to the trail.

Shadows were long on the dirt street when he rode down it. This wasn't a secret visit; nor did he want it to be a long one. Mason just wanted to see if there was anything he should know before being committed to a shoot-out . . . and he wanted to stay clear of trouble.

Murtry stood in the stable door, waved Mason through it, and followed the dun to a stall.

"Whatcha doin' in town? Figured you'd be stayin' kinda close to your men bein's it's gittin close to trail drive time."

"Yeah, reckon I ought to, but I figured maybe it'd be a good idea to know what's happened in here." He glanced at Murtry. "Reckon you heard about Hamilton gunning old Sam Sisson?"

"Uh-huh, I heard. The whole town's heard. Hamilton told it. Said Sam drawed on 'im and he had to kill 'im."

"Sisson's not dead, Murtry."

"Wh-why—"

"Yeah, it'd figure Hamilton would think he killed him, the way the bullet took him in the head, but Sisson's a rugged old man. He is a long way from dead. Matter of fact he's up and around like nothin' ever happened."

"Damn! I'm right glad to hear that. Reckon I oughtta be tellin' the town folks; they been nigh on ready to string Hamilton up. 'Bout the only thing's kept 'em from it is Slade's fast guns hangin' around town. Come on back, I'll pour you a cup of coffee, and you can tell me about it."

The coffee was hot and thick. Mason drank a few swallows, then looked at Murtry. He shook his head. "I'll tell you about it shortly, but first, it might be a good idea not to tell the town folks that Sisson's all right. Let 'em stay mad awhile. It's in their interest to get rid of the Hamilton and Slade bunch as much as it is in the ranchers'."

At Murtry's frown, Mason continued. "Ah, c'mon, old-timer, I'm not trying to trick these people. They just need to stay mad long enough to know what side they're on." He walked to a bale of hay and sat. "Now I'll tell you about Sisson getting shot—the way it really happened."

When he'd told the whole story, leaving out his part in nursing Sisson back to health, he looked, narrow-eyed, at Murtry. "I'm convinced more than ever Slade and Hamilton are in this together, but no proof we could take to the law— if we had any law."

Not thinking, he pulled his right-hand .44 and inspected it for dust, and seeing it was all right, he repeated the performance with his left gun. "It's coming down to a big shoot-out, Murtry, and some people are gonna get hurt. I hate like hell to see it happen, but if these folks are going to live with any dignity, or self-respect, it's got to be. Those who don't want a fight will leave anyway."

Murtry nodded. "Reckon you're right, young'un, but I believe they's somethin' you oughtta know—these folks done made up their mind. They're ready to fight now they got a leader. Shore am glad you showed up in this here valley when you did."

"I am too, Murtry." He stood. "Think I'll go see Barkley. Feel like a beer would taste pretty good. You want one?"

"Got a couple things I need to take care of here first. Horses need feedin' and waterin'. You go ahead. I'll be down in a minute. Fer's I know, most a Slade's gunhawks done left town for the ranch, but be careful anyway."

Mason nodded, knowing as he walked out that Murtry had noticed he'd not thumbed the thongs over the hammers of his guns.

Through with walking in the shadows and down back alleys, Mason walked boldly down the boardwalk. Before entering the saloon, he swept a glance along the tie rail in front. There were five Box S horses tied there. He eased the .44s in their holsters and pushed through the doors.

He walked along the wall, eyes searching, and noted where each Slade rider sat. By the time he reached the corner of the bar and leaned against the wall, he knew where they all were.

Not waiting for Mason to ask, Barkley slid a cold beer down the bar to him. Deftly catching the handle with his left hand, Mason brought the mug to his lips and swallowed. His gaze still searched above its rim.

Chet Cassidy, one of Slade's riders, walked to the bar, to Mason's right. "You got no trouble with me, Cole. I know I ain't fast enough to shade you on the draw an' I don't hunt in a pack. Whatever they do, leave me out of it."

Mason's gaze locked with Cassidy's. He stared silently a moment and knew the man spoke the truth. "All right. I'm not hunting trouble, but if your friends bring it to me, I'll deal you out."

Cassidy nodded and stepped down the bar a few paces.

"Well, I ain't yeller," a short, weazle-faced gunman spoke up. "You got trouble with me—and these other three. Think you can get us all?"

Mason let a soft smile break the corners of his lips. "Now I don't know whether I'll get all of you, but I'll get at least three—and you'll be the first down."

He saw doubt replace bluster in the weazle's face. From the corner of his eye he saw Barkley slide his double-barreled twelve-gauge to the counter.

"You're not gonna shoot up my saloon. If you rannies want trouble with Mason, you'll go out on the street one at a time to face him." Barkley moved the business end of the twelve-gauge, slowly sweeping the crowd with it. "Make up your minds right now."

Mason kept his eyes on the weazle, and saw his hand dip, fast, real fast, for his gun. Mason's right hand never seemed to move, yet his .44 was spitting fire.

The barrel of the weazle's pistol not yet clear of leather, he stood staring at Mason from unbelieving eyes, then looked down at his chest. Two holes, close enough together for a silver dollar to cover them, were in the middle, between his two pockets. He again looked at Mason, tried to say something, folded at the waist, and fell forward.

Mason leaned on the bar and casually waved his .44 in the direction of the other three. "Unless you want some of the same, drag your friend outta here so he doesn't bleed all over Barkley's floor."

One of the three, hands held clear of his guns, bent over his friend. His eyes were wide, as if he couldn't believe what he'd seen. "Mister, you got no trouble with me. I ain't never seen a draw and shoot fast as you." He twisted to look at the other two Slade men. "We should've left like the others, when we found out who he was." The ranny reached down and placing his hands under the shoulders of the dead man, lifted, and dragged him toward the door.

"We're drawing our time," one of the two remaining punchers said. "Slade ain't got enough money to make us face you."

"That's your affair," Mason said. "Now, help get that two-bit gunslinger out of here, and keep riding or I'll put you on the same train to hell he's riding." He glanced at Barkley. "Sorry. He brought it to me. I didn't want it to happen in your place."

"*De nada,* 'tis nothing," Barkley repeated in English. "For a second there I thought I was gonna have to *help* you mess it up."

The first puncher who'd dealt himself out of the gunplay spoke up. "Just so's you know, I ain't working for Slade no more either. Gonna leave here, draw my time, and hit the trail. Maybe I'll live to tell my grand-babies how smart I was the time I almost had to face Cole." He downed his drink, flipped Barkley a two-bit piece, and walked out.

The doors hadn't stopped swinging when Murtry entered, almost running. "What'd I miss—hot dammit! What'd I miss?"

Barkley threw back his head and guffawed. Mason smiled stiffly. He punched the spent brass from the cylinder of his gun and replaced it with new loads.

He'd not realized until then that every man in the saloon seemed to be talking at once. Times past he would have turned and walked out, leaving them to wonder about him, but too many now knew who he was, so he stayed to listen to Barkley tell Murtry what he'd missed.

"Well," Mason cut in on Barkley's description of the action, "one good thing came out of this—Slade's got four less gunhawks than he had this morning—no, five less. I forgot about the one who dealt himself out before anything happened."

Mason glanced at Murtry. "You leave the dun saddled like I asked? I figured to leave after talking with Barkley, but now I reckon I'll wait until morning." He drank the rest of his beer and asked for two more, one for Murtry and one for himself. "How 'bout you strip my rig off him, rub 'im down, give 'im some grain, and I'll get him in the morning? I'm tired—these things always leave me drained."

"Yeah, I'll take care of him. What time you want 'im in the mornin', 'bout daylight maybe? I'll have 'im ready for you."

Mason nodded, then glanced at Barkley. "Sorry, Barkley. I didn't offer you a drink. Reckon I forgot my manners."

"Think nothing of it. Yeah, I'll have one, and I'll buy a round before you go."

While they finished their drinks, Mason noticed, Barkley kept a sharp watch on the door—and he didn't put the shotgun under the bar.

"Think I'll see if the hotel's full," Mason said. "Gonna get a night's sleep. Don't know when I'll get another." He thanked Barkley again for backing him, and left.

He woke earlier than he wanted, but he went down, ate breakfast, and collected his horse from the livery. He watched the sun come up after two hours on the trail.

On the way, his searching gaze saw deer and antelope tracks, and a pretty good-sized bear had passed this way. It had clawed the bark well up the trunk of a tree. Mason came to an antelope carcass, about half-devoured. Mountain lion, he thought. "Reckon I scared him off." The dun shied at the scent of the fresh kill.

Mason worked his way down a dry draw and up the other side. His ranch was just over the next rise. He had to hold the big dun back—he wanted to run. Like all horses, he knew where home was and needed no urging. Finally Mason let him take the bit and run.

When he topped out on the rise, he saw Jaime Martinez on the other side of the outbuildings, riding as if he'd just heard the chow bell. Mason knew it was Martinez from the way he sat his saddle. No one rode as gracefully as that vaquero. They reached the stable at the same time.

"*Buenos dias,* amigo," Mason said. "What's the hurry?"

"I theenk Slade ees feexin to move the herd, amigo. The chuck wagon's already pulled out."

"All right!" This was the moment he'd waited for. "Send riders to the other ranches, but first be sure they all have plenty of rifle and pistol ammunition. They won't be coming back this way until it's over, and tell them to make sure the riders from the other ranches have plenty of loads for their guns too."

"Sí, you want me weeth you?" Martinez slung the words over his shoulder as he headed for the bunkhouse.

"Yeah," Mason yelled, "and tell them to be sure they are not seen—ride the low country until they get to the canyon."

Mason packed quickly. As an extra precaution, he rolled a packet of lucifers in oilskin, wanting to be doubly sure he could light the dynamite. It might be the difference in this shoot-out.

When finished, he went back to the stable and saddled the black. Martinez was pulling the cinch straps on his saddle tight. Mason, as he had many times in the past, glanced at Martinez's horse and thought that it had about as much Morgan blood as his own black.

"We'll leave soon's you're ready. Want to get to the canyon a couple of days ahead of the herd." He pushed his hat back off his brow and leaned against the black. "Way I figure, it'll take the herd about three days to reach the mouth of the canyon. We can be there in one, and you and I have some work to do before they reach it." He stepped into the stirrups. "Let's ride."

From the moment they rode off, they scouted for sign of Slade riders. The most danger they'd have of being seen would be when they came close to the herd, but they would have to take that chance in order to reach the canyon ahead of it.

Mason led them down sandy creek beds, around stark, rocky hills, up shallow ravines and dry washes—wherever there was cover, he used it. They rode into a heavy stand of aspen, and

Mason signaled a halt. The horses needed a breather.

"I theenk maybe not even the Apache could follow you, amigo," Martinez said, a note of admiration in his voice.

"There've been times I've had to prove that," Mason said. "We should be coming on the herd anytime now, so we'll have to be even more careful. Don't want to ride after dark, but if we can pass the herd far enough, we might chance it." He climbed back in the saddle. "Let's go."

Mason saw trail dust roiling above the crests of the hills long before he heard the lowing of the cows and yelling of the trail crew. He twisted in his saddle.

"I'm gonna take a close look, see how many men they have and how far the herd's strung out."

Dismounting, he motioned Martinez to do the same; then, holding the black's reins, he crouched and ran toward the crest. Before topping out, he ground-reined the black and dropped to his stomach.

Stretched full-length, Mason pulled himself along by his elbows until he could see in both directions. He stopped and felt Martinez slither alongside.

The drag riders were pushing the rear of the herd pretty hard, so as to keep them bunched, but even with that the herd stretched about two miles from point to drag.

Straining his eyes, Mason tried to see through the dust to the other side of the herd, but could see nothing. He counted the riders closest to him and estimated, with a like number on the other side and allowing for drag and point riders, there must be about twenty-five in all. He'd seen what he'd come to see. Nudging Martinez, he started backing down the hill.

They retrieved their horses and climbed aboard.

"How many men you figure they have with them, Martinez?"

"Maybe twenty-five. What you theenk?"

" 'Bout what I figure. Now, we better put some distance between us an' that herd."

The trail to the canyon rim was rugged. Erosion had cut deep ravines, rockfall was common, and old blowdowns stacked trees into barricades that sometimes stretched a quarter of a mile. They all had to be skirted.

Mason set a slow pace, not taking a chance on crippling the big black. He stopped frequently to rest the horses, for the grade was steep. Here on the side of the mountain he selected their rest sites carefully; a chance look would reveal them to those below.

Topping out on the canyon rim, they saw ahead of them, about a quarter-mile, a heavy blowdown. Upon reaching it, they circled to go around.

"We'll have a fire and hot food tonight, Martinez. Let's make camp here." Mason reined in, dismounted, and took care of his horse.

"You deserve a rest, old boy, and this grass up here looks tender and juicy. Was gonna ride you over to the rim, but you take it easy."

The big horse swung his head and looked at him. His snort sounded like a thank you to Mason.

Mason looked at Martinez. "You go ahead and start supper. I'm gonna walk over and have a look at the canyon."

Mason removed his boots and put his moccasins on, then headed for the rim.

Although there was little chance anyone would see him, he used his customary caution. It paid off.

Squirming close enough to peer into the canyon, Mason saw two riders directly below him, walking their horses toward the canyon exit, the end at which the herd would leave the valley. They talked, and Mason heard them clearly. The canyon walls channeled sound to him.

"I don't rightly know what the hell Slade wanted us to scout this canyon for," one of them growled. Mason couldn't tell which one was talking. "They ain't been nobody through here since we brung the last herd this way."

"Aw, you know how he is. He don't want no hitches in this. Besides, he's been awful skittish since he found out he was buckin' Cole. C'mon, we'll git fer enough to see the end and turn back. It'll be another day, maybe a day and a half, fore Slade gits the herd this far . . ."

Their voices faded as they rode out of earshot. Mason eased back from his vantage point and stood. He hit a long ground-eating stride in the direction Slade's riders were heading. He wanted another look at that end of the canyon. The dog-leg to the right prevented him from studying it as thoroughly as he wished.

After maybe a quarter of an hour, he judged he was far enough past the bend to allow him the view he needed. He went to his belly again and crawled to the rim for another look.

Slade's riders would again be riding toward him, for he'd cut straight across the angle of the bend and was now ahead of them. The walls were not as high here; they sloped off to cut through rolling hills. The riders apparently saw this too.

"This's far enough," one of them said. "Let's make camp an' head back to the herd in the morning."

Mason watched them build a fire and start their evening meal. Every so often he shifted his gaze, not wanting them to feel his look. To men like that, a gaze was almost as physical as a touch.

They'd made camp well back from the exit. In fact, they were about at the very point Mason figured to set the dynamite charges, and now that he'd seen it up close, he was satisfied his plan would work.

He offered a silent prayer that it could be done without more killing, on either side, but was not convinced that that was possible.

He ran back to camp. He felt good, totally alive. After days of hard riding, he felt his leg and back muscles flex and stretch and become limber. Sweat trickled down his forehead and into his eyes; it flowed between his shoulders and soaked his shirt. His breathing was strong and unlabored. He had many times run for hours, and each time it gave him a sense of freedom unequaled by any other experience.

As he drew close to camp, he saw that Martinez had a fire burning, and there was no smoke rising from it. Mason smiled. Martinez was pretty good at playing Indian also. Smoke would settle in the canyon and possibly alert those down below that they were not alone.

They ate the usual for supper: hardtack, beans, bacon, and coffee. After eating, Mason went to his saddlebags and withdrew a tin of peaches, cut the top from it, and handed the tin to Martinez.

White teeth flashed. Martinez stuck his knife into a half of a peach, sucked the juice from it, and then ate it slowly. "Amigo, you're a good friend. Who else would share such a treat?"

Mason said nothing. His mouth filled with peach, he just grinned.

The peaches finished, Mason poured them each another cup of coffee, then sipped at the strong, hot brew and watched the sun sink behind the crests. When the shadows painted the land a soft purple, he crawled into his blankets and joined Martinez in sleep.

12

MASON OPENED HIS eyes and lay still, getting the feel of his surroundings. He looked at the sky, judged it to be about five o'clock, groaned, and slipped out of his blankets. Martinez was up and had the fire started. Mason untied the picket ropes, moved the horses to fresh grass, and turned back toward camp, stopping to breathe deeply.

Crisp morning air, mingled with the aroma of fresh-brewed coffee and fried beans, caused him to smile. He thought, City folks can have their little world of dust, dirt, rotting garbage, and unwashed bodies. They don't know what living is all about.

Martinez handed him a steaming cup of coffee when he walked into the ring of firelight. He nodded his thanks.

"I think we'll leave the cache of dynamite where it is until the others get here," Mason said, more to himself than to Martinez. He looked up. "You and I can take what we need with us. I want to set a charge on each side of the canyon, far enough back from the mouth to make sure we block the trail wall to wall."

He knew if they blocked the canyon, he and the ranchers would have a much longer drive ahead of them when they marketed *their* cattle, but he saw no other choice if they were going to beat Slade.

He took a swallow of coffee and grimaced. "Whew! That's hot. Must have been close to the fire; it burned all the way down. But back to the dynamite, there's no hurry. We'll have to wait until those two riders break camp and are far enough gone so we'll not be seen or heard."

They finished their coffee, put out the fire, and cleaned the camp before riding to the tarp-covered cache. When Mason was satisfied that they had enough dynamite, caps, and fuse, he divided it. And then they tied it, the hand sledge and star drill, to the back of their saddles' cantles. They then secured the remainder under the tarp and left.

"I want to be sure those riders are well around the bend before we get hung out to dry in plain sight. We'll make a target hard to miss, hanging down those walls on a rope."

Again, Mason slipped off his horse and snaked up to the canyon. He saw only empty trail and studied it closely. There were no large rocks that could hide two riders, so they must have still been encamped, or coming toward him from the dog-leg end.

"I think we'll just wait until they get this far," he said, "then we'll go ahead with our work."

The sun pushed the night chill into the shadows. The warmth between his shoulders felt good. Mason flexed his back muscles to take away the aching cold and relaxed against the ground, thinking it might be a long wait.

He squirmed. They had a lot of work ahead, and every minute they were forced to wait here made the workday longer. Then he saw the lead horse appear and off his flank came the other. Now they could get started. He watched until the riders were another couple hundred yards up-canyon, then signaled Martinez to bring the horses.

They reined in at the rim. Mason looked closely at each wall and charted the spots where the charges had to be placed.

"I think it'd be better if we work together and do one side at a time. What's your thinking on it?"

"I theenk you are right, amigo. Eet weel be safer, and maybe faster."

Mason swung his leg up over the pommel, then slipped from the saddle. Martinez followed suit, and they began off-loading the equipment.

"Two charges on each side should block any chance of the herd getting through," Mason said. "One about halfway down and one near the top on each side." He looked at Martinez to see if he agreed.

"Sí." Martinez nodded. "And eet looks like there ees a narrow ledge across the way there, but on thees side weel be hanging from a rope. I'll take thees side first, amigo."

"No, I had some training in this sort of thing when I was at the Point, I'd better do it."

They worked quietly but steadily for about forty-five minutes, tying the rope into a sling that would afford as much
comfort, and safety, as possible under the circumstances. The
last knot tied, Mason again pulled at each of them, making
certain they'd not loosen and drop Martinez or him into the
bottom of the canyon.

"I think that'll do it." He adjusted the sling around his waist
and seat, then went to the black and looped the rope a couple
of turns around his saddle horn.

"I believe anchored to the horn like this'll make it quick
to pull me up—if we have to. I'll take the star drill and
hand sledge down with me. Lower the dynamite and other
stuff when I signal for it." He looked at Martinez. "Lower it
carefully, amigo—very carefully."

"Ah, señor, you sure you don't want me to save time and
drop eet to you? Eet weel be much faster," Martinez joked.

Mason clutched Martinez's shoulder. "Let's get the job
done. We've already lost a lot of time. That herd's moving
slow—but they were moving while we waited for those riders
to clear the area."

Mason slipped over the edge as Martinez slowly fed out rope
from around the saddle horn.

Mason squirmed his hips in the rope saddle. It felt pretty
good right now, but he knew that after he had hung in it for a
while, each twist and knot would bite into his flesh, cutting off
circulation and pulling skin into blisters. It would be torture.

Slipping slowly down the face of the cliff, Mason studied
it for cracks and crevices. Sometimes, the various stratum
would be separated, leaving a natural hole in which to plant
the dynamite charges, and he hoped to luck out and find such
a hole.

Only a few feet short of halfway down the face of the cliff,
Mason found what he was looking for, a thin crevice between
two layers of strata. Good, this'll work in our favor, he thought,
and signaled Martinez to stop lowering.

He placed the star drill against the face of the cliff and
tapped it lightly with the hand sledge. It bit into the sandstone
easily. His next blow was harder, but still a test as to how hard
he'd have to swing. Now he knew and went to work in earnest,
thinking he wouldn't have been surprised to find granite here;
then he really would have had a day's work cut out for him.

He opened a hole as deep as his arm could reach, large enough for five sticks of the explosive. He set the charge, connected the fuse, and studied his handiwork a moment. Can't leave it like this, he thought, it'll blow straight out of the hole.

He chipped several chunks of the soft stone and wedged them into the hole, then chipped smaller pieces and pushed them in behind the larger ones. He knew that mud tamped in there would have been better, but this would have to do.

Looking up, he saw Martinez, rope in hand, peering down at him.

"All right, pull me up a ways. I might as well set the other charge while I'm down here."

Sweat and dust streaked his face. Each knot and braid of rope etched his flesh, but too much time would be lost if he had Martinez pull him up. Then more time would be lost in lowering Martinez.

He was not as lucky with this charge. He had no crevice to start the drill into. Hit, twist, hit, twist, hit, twist—it seemed he made little progress.

The hole was still only about a foot deep. The heavy sledge hammer had taken its toll. His right shoulder felt like lead. He shifted the sledge to his left hand in order to rest the shoulder, but then his strokes didn't hit the drill with the accuracy he'd had with his right hand.

He swung, and despite the hurt and leaden feeling of his shoulder, he decided to take one more hard swing before again shifting hands.

The drill pulled off to the right and—he hit his right hand. As soon as the sledge smashed his fist against the cliff, Mason knew he wouldn't be handling a handgun for a couple of weeks, maybe longer.

A glance showed him that Martinez had not seen what happened. He decided to say nothing about it.

Another look at the hole, and he decided to use it as it was, hoping it was deep enough. He set the charge and signaled Martinez to pull him up.

He didn't know whether the rope digging into his flesh or his sorely bruised, maybe broken, hand was causing him the most pain, but he shrugged it off, for now it seemed his entire body hurt just as bad.

Reaching the top, he rolled onto his back and tried to pull his legs under him to stand, but they wouldn't obey. He lay still a few moments, breathing deeply, then started trying to knead life back into his legs.

He hid his right hand under his legs while rubbing with his left. He would keep it in his pocket while talking to Martinez or others. He worked with one leg while Martinez massaged the other. Mason suppressed a groan; circulation was returning, and the tingling felt as though needles were being driven into every pore.

He looked at Martinez. "You will set but one charge on the other side, amigo. I'll set the other."

When Martinez started to protest, Mason held up his hand.

"No. It'll be as I say. If we had to leave here right now, in a hurry, we'd be buzzard bait before you could get me on a horse; it is best we do it my way."

"Sí." Martinez nodded.

Mason saw he'd not fooled Martinez, that he knew he was trying to spare him pain.

It didn't take long for the feeling to return to Mason's legs. They again loaded the gear on the horses, threaded their way down the mountain, and no more than reached the bottom before they started to climb the other side.

"There have been a lot of cows driven through this canyon," Mason said thoughtfully, looking at the deeply worn trail.

"Sí, that trail has been churned by many a hoof. Eet has been used hard." Martinez reined his horse around a boulder. "We must stop Slade thees time. I don't theenk the ranchers weel have the heart to keep fighting."

He slanted a look at Mason. "Eef eet was not for you, señor, I theenk they would already have quit."

"We'll stop him, Martinez—we'll stop him for good."

He reined the black in, swung to the ground, and walked over to look toward the bottom of the canyon. The walls were straight up and down, but not quite as high on this side.

After unloading the horses, Martinez picked up the rope and started to shrug into it, making ready to go over the side.

"No, hold up awhile," Mason said. "We need something to tamp in on top of the charge. Let's take care of that before you go down."

His gaze searched the slope, and he saw a small stream about a hundred yards farther up. Such streams usually had rock or clay beds—Mason hoped for the latter.

He wished for a bucket, but took the coffee pot instead. These streams were mostly from snow melt. This one had cut its way through the claylike topsoil and was flowing on gravel and rock-slab, but Mason was interested in the topsoil along the bank.

He dug out a handful, wet it, and pushed it into the bottom of the coffee pot. He repeated the process until the pot was full. "This should be enough," he said. "Won't take much to direct the force of the explosion against the rock. After you set the charge, I'll lower the pot to you."

They worked silently. Each knew what he had to do and went about doing it. Mason's hand was badly swollen by now, and he had trouble keeping Martinez from noticing while he set his charge. By mid-afternoon they were through. They hadn't stopped for a nooning, so they chewed strips of jerky while they worked.

Mason leaned tiredly against his horse and saw Martinez doing the same. They were both dirty and sweaty, but Mason was satisfied, as a man tends to be after completing a hard job, having done it well.

They looked at each other, fatigue showing plainly on their faces.

"Let's head for camp, amigo. The others should start drifting in anytime now." Mason grasped the apple with his left hand and swung aboard.

Shadows were long and the air cool by the time they rode into camp. More than half of the ranchers and their men were present, and in the distance Mason saw others approaching. Brody told Mason that his outfit had been one of the first to arrive.

Mason's cook, Ed Tomlinson, had brought everything he would need to feed them. Time and secrecy had not permitted use of a chuck wagon, so Tomlinson had used two pack horses. He was now busy getting supper going, but already had a large kettle of coffee brewed.

Mason stripped the hull off his horse, picketed him for the night, and poured himself a cup of coffee. He slouched on the ground by his saddle, intending to wait until all had arrived before talking of tomorrow's plan.

He dozed, and when next he sipped his coffee, it was cold. Looking around, he saw that everyone had arrived, including Bryson and Sisson.

Mason wished in his heart that they hadn't come, but he knew it would be a terrible blow to their manhood to tell them to stay out of the fight.

He stood, poured another cup of coffee, and had started to motion the ranchers and their hands around him when he saw Sisson nod that he wanted to talk. He walked to him, and Sisson took his elbow to lead him away from the others.

"Got somethin' I want to say, boy. Don't need nobody but you to hear it."

"All right, Sisson." Mason gave him a look. "You feelin' all right since you got shot?"

Sisson made a chopping motion with his right hand. "Why hell, boy, ain't no one slug gonna put me down for good, but enough of that. I want you to know something.

"Reckon you know I ain't got no family, nobody who gives a damn about me, or the ranch, 'cept you and Laura, and the boys, of course. Well," he continued, "gittin' shot like I did got me to thinkin', what's gonna happen to my ranch when I finally cut out?"

He squinted at Mason to see if he was listening. "Aw now, I ain't figurin' on cashing in my chips anytime soon, but when it does happen—well, I done wrote it all down an' took it in to the lawyer man in town an' made it all legal-like . . ."

"What're you talking about, Sisson?" Mason looked at him through narrowed eyes, trying to see clearly in the darkness closing about them.

"Well, it's like this. I'm givin' you and Laura the ranch—no, I don't want to hear no protest. I own every foot of it. I ain't leasin' no gov'ment land.

"It borders on the Larsen place, and will make you and Laura a place big enough to raise a dozen or so kids. When this is over I'd kinda like for you two to come over and go over my books with me."

He turned loose of Mason's arm and belted him on the shoulder. "Hey! You and Laura are like my own kids." Mason heard him sort of choke up, and didn't look directly at him for fear of embarrassing him.

"Now I done talked to all my men. Hell, they're 'bout as old as me, and they thought it would be great to have you young folks around. So no arguin'. It's all settled."

"Sisson—I don't know what to say. It just doesn't seem right for me to come into the valley and have this happen."

"Then don't say nothin'. You're the only man I ever seen that I figured would run it the way I would, and would fight for it if need be—and win. That's what's important—havin' the guts to fight for what's your'n and keeping it. What you've done for this bunch here, I don't believe there's another man anywhere that could have done it. So 'nuff said. Right, boy?"

Mason grasped Sisson's shoulder and squeezed. He didn't say anything. There were times when words could not say what one wanted to say, and besides, he didn't think he could get a word past the lump in his throat. They walked slowly back to camp.

When Mason got back to the fire, he tossed his cold coffee on the fire and called the men around him.

He told them in detail what they would have to do on the morrow, and while telling them, he looked each in the eyes, one after the other, silently, solemnly. He didn't remind them that this time the next day some of them might not be around— they knew that.

"Men, Martinez and I will blow the charges at the end of the canyon. We'll wait until the point riders are almost upon us. The drag should be almost a mile into the canyon by then. Don't fire until you hear the explosion, then fire a few shots into the air to let them know they're under attack."

He stared at the ground a moment, then again looked at the men. "I just can't bring myself to ambush anybody. Anyway, if they return your fire, then make your shots count.

"I think they'll run; if they do, let them go." He paced in front of them. "Remember, though, if you have to kill them— they brought this fight to you. They came in here and stole from you, threatened you, and took advantage of their gun skills to throw fear for your families into all of you.

"I don't like it any more than you, but show no mercy— it might get you killed." He stopped pacing and faced them. "Any questions?"

They were quiet, sober, but as Mason looked at them, he detected no fear, just a quiet resolution to get the job done.

"All right, let's bed down. Tomorrow'll be a long day." He walked toward his saddle, then turned back. "One more thing, after the herd stampedes and is out of the canyon, scatter them as much as possible, then head for your homes.

"I'm going to end this whole thing tomorrow or the next day, going to town when I leave here." Then, looking at each in turn, he said, "Brody, Brannigan, Martinez, I want you to side me. The rest of you head back to the ranch."

Then, including the whole group, he explained, "I think Slade will head for town after we rout him here. If I'm right he'll want to talk to his partner, and I'll be there to greet him."

Mason lay awake long after the camp was quiet. He knew they had no choice in what they were about to do. It was this or pack up and move on. He could ask the territorial governor in Santa Fe for troops, but there wasn't enough time for them to get there. The valley was surrounded by mountains, and between it and Santa Fe lay many of the San Juan range's most rugged peaks, making the route tortuous.

The night sounds, a faint smell of dust, and the softness of night closed around him. He slept.

Mason opened his eyes. The men were beginning to stir. Tomlinson was up and had breakfast cooking. He lay still a moment, thinking. This was the day everything would be settled.

He rolled over and stood, flexing his muscles, trying to work the chill out of his body. Then he looked at his right hand. It was swollen such that he couldn't close his fist, couldn't grip a handgun, let alone fire it.

Well, I took this job on, and come what will I'm going to finish it, he thought. He walked to the fire and poured a cup of coffee. Tomlinson handed him a plate of beans and bacon. Mason nodded his thanks and sat down to eat. He didn't speak—words were for when you had something to say.

The camp came to life slowly. Mason watched. There was no reason to hurry; it would take the herd some time to snake its way deep into the canyon.

When finally all had eaten and policed the area, Mason stood.

"One last thing, men," he said, calling for their attention, "each of you take a couple sticks of dynamite, and when the herd starts folding back on itself, blow your sticks right where it's folding. Now, you better get riding. I'll take my signal from those on this side."

He pushed his hat to the back of his head and squinted thoughtfully. "If I have Slade figured right, he's gonna take as many men into town with him as will go. Those that don't stay with him will just keep going on out of the valley when we get through here today.

"You—Brody, Brannigan, Martinez—just cover my back when we get there." Then to the group in general, he said, "Don't any of you expose yourselves to Slade's gunfire unless you have to. We have the advantage of both surprise and position. I don't want any of you hurt. All right, let's move out."

Mason watched them ride off in small bunches, then turned again to Martinez. "You take the other side. I'll signal when to set off your charges. *Bueno suerte,* amigo."

"Good luck to you, too, my friend."

They separated, two proud fighting men, to do a job that had to be done if decent men and women were to be allowed to work, live, and love in this beautiful country.

Mason reined in far enough from the edge so he would not be skylined, and swung down from the black. He looked back toward the others taking their positions. From his vantage point he saw each group and wanted to make sure he could see the last man, the one closest to the entrance. It was from him he'd get the signal that the drag had entered the canyon.

He swiped at a troublesome fly. Time seemed to stop. Finally he saw the dot he knew to be a man move back from the edge, take off his hat, and wave it in a circling motion. The herd was in the canyon.

He flopped to his belly and snaked up to peer into the emptiness below. Not yet. There was no sign of the point riders. He raised his head and looked across. Martinez was there in much the same position as he. They waited.

First, Mason heard the rumble of the thousands of hooves beating the earth to fine powder, then the yells of the trail hands. He shook his head, his heart heavy with what they were about to do.

Most of those men below were good cowhands, but somewhere along their backtrail they had taken the wrong fork, the easy dollar had looked too good. Given the chance, some would still make it in a law-abiding society, most would not.

There were many cattlemen who'd been careless about whose cows they dropped their rope on, especially over in Texas after the War Between the States, when herds had gone wild. Those men had turned back and taken the straight trail.

Mason shrugged mentally. There were times that he had come close, too close, to taking the easy way. The point rider came into view, breaking into his thoughts. He looked across at Martinez and shook his head. Not yet.

He waited until the lead steer was almost straight below, then nodded and lit the fuse. Martinez followed suit, then stood and ran for cover. Mason did the same, not knowing how much of where he had been lying would end up in the bottom of the canyon.

He squatted behind a large boulder. After a few seconds, he felt the earth under him tremble and convulse. Looking toward the rim, he saw the ground rise and then fall away. Both sides exploded upward and outward at the same time. He edged closer to the rim and looked down into a roiling cloud of dust, and out of it he heard the bawling of fear-crazed cattle.

He sprang to the back of the black and headed for the other end at a dead run, wanting to see what was happening below. Every few hundred yards, he reined his horse to the edge and looked over. Finally, the cloud of dust thinned enough that he could see.

The cows in front of the herd had turned and were trying to climb over the tons of beef still being carried forward by those behind.

Mason lit another stick of dynamite and dropped it into the churning mass below. More cows tried to turn; some didn't make it, for as soon as they were broadside to the charging mass, horns and hooves plowed them to the ground.

Mason hated that it had to be this way, but the herd must be turned and stampeded toward the entrance. The sooner they were, the fewer cows would die.

The sharp crack of rifle fire came from the end of the herd. Slade's men were in the middle of an earthly hell, cows overrunning them. The sights and sounds of men screaming, bullets, cows, dust, blood and guts, all mingled, such that Mason figured hell's inferno would be tame by comparison.

He knew what fear could do to men. He'd seen brave men caught up in the contagion of fear unleashed by hopelessness—at Appomattox, Shelbyville, Gettysburg, and too many other places where men had died, screaming out their fear in anger.

He kicked his horse into a full run, wanting to be at the canyon entrance when Slade's people emerged.

The herd was now in an all-out stampede back the way they'd come. Mason passed groups of men and motioned them to follow.

When he reached the entrance, he was too late. The herd was flowing from it, as heedless of barriers, man, or nature, as a river of molten lava. He saw some of Slade's men ahead of the herd, not trying to stem the stampede, intent only on escape.

He reined in, as did the riders behind him. There was nothing to do but let the stampede run its course. There was no danger from Slade's men, for they would have to fall back and reorganize, and Mason thought this attack might have hurt them so bad as to make that unlikely.

The Snake foreman sat his horse next to him, his leg hooked over the saddle horn.

"Chisolm, I'm going on into town. As soon as Martinez can cross behind the herd, tell him, Brody, and Brannigan to come on in. They know what to do.

"The rest of you better head for home. I don't believe Slade's people are in any shape to cause you trouble—but just in case."

He pulled his horse around, then turned back. "A couple of other things. Before you cut out, have the men make a sweep of the canyon. There may be some poor devil in there, wounded or stomped and needing help.

"I've already made a count of our people. Thank God, we didn't lose any. And one other thing, make damned sure Sisson goes home with you, if you have to hogtie him."

"That'll be the day." Chisolm cast him a sour look.

Mason raised his eyebrows, then nodded at Chisolm's words. "This *is* the day, Chisolm. We'll all remember it the rest of our lives, and most won't remember it with pride, but only as the day a job that had to be done was done, and the way we did it seemed the only way."

Mason pulled the black around and headed for town, knowing there was much yet to be done before this day could be counted a victory.

He looked at his hand and tried to flex his fingers. They would not close. They were swollen such that they felt hot, and the skin was tight around them, as if it would split if he did manage to bend them, even a little. His whole hand, starting at his wrist, was a deep purple, almost black. He shook his head, wondering if it was broken.

Barkley, Murtry, Martinez, Brody . . . hell, he could count on the whole town to take on the fight if he showed them what had happened, but this was his fight, and he'd not let another man get killed trying to help him.

He raised his eyes to the trail ahead, wondering if its end would also be his end.

13

RIDING TOWARD PERHAPS the most dangerous gunfight of his life, and certainly the most important, Mason again held his right hand out in front of him. It took only a glance to show that it was still as swollen and blue as when he'd last looked. He'd not expected different.

He tried to flex his fingers, but they'd close only a little. He was well aware that time and events would not permit the inevitable to be put off. He was going to fight Slade, and if he came through that, he'd still have Hamilton to face.

Letting his horse set his own pace, Mason hooked his leg around the saddle horn and wished for a cigar. He had found that a good smoke was a companionable way to pass the time and to think. He needed time now to figure some way to delay what was coming.

His stomach growled, and glancing at the sun, he realized it was well past noon and he'd not eaten. A stand of pines drew his attention, and he saw a small stream to the side of them. He didn't reckon that the world was going to end if he took time to fix a little grub. Hate to get shot with an empty stomach, he thought and then frowned, wondering what gave him the idea he was going to get shot.

He rode into the pines, dismounted, and took his cooking gear from behind the saddle. After scraping needles from the area, he built a small fire and put a pot of water on for coffee. Then he opened a tin of beans, put bacon in them, and set the can next to the fire to warm.

Waiting for his food to heat, Mason watered his horse again, then walked upstream, knelt, and drank his fill. He walked back to the fire and sat leaning against the bole of a large pine, trying to think of a way to buy time in order to tend to his hand.

A glance at the fire showed the coffee water boiling. He stood, walked over, and dumped grounds into the pot. His beans and bacon were warm, ready to eat.

While slowly eating from the tin, he again pondered his problem. The beans were almost gone when suddenly he smiled. It just might work, he thought and stood to go.

The shadows grew long, then merged into the purples and midnight blues of dusk before Mason saw the lights of Rock Creek spread ahead of him.

The livery stable was always dark, except for the lantern hanging over the big double doors in front and the one in Murtry's room. Like most stables, the livery also had double doors in back. These were the ones Mason used.

Being quieter than usual, he was almost through rubbing his horse down before he heard Murtry leave his room and walk toward him.

"Shhh," Mason said. "Don't do anything to indicate you just took in a boarder. Go back to your room and turn the lantern down, or out, and drop your curtain over the window. I'll be there in a minute."

Murtry did an about-face and went to his room with not a word.

The big horse taken care of, Mason slipped from the stall, first making sure that no one was approaching the stable. He shadowed his way into Murtry's room. It was dark.

"What's going on?" Murtry whispered.

"Murtry, I need to buy some time." Although not whispering, Mason's voice was so soft it could be heard only in the room. "When you get back, I'll tell you everything that's happened today, but first there's something I want you to do for me."

"All right. You said when I get back, so where am I goin'?"

"First, go tell Barkley to send word to Slade that I'll meet him in four days. I'll give him that much time to decide if he wants to lose everything. Tell him, the only thing he's taking with him will be a chunk of lead—a .44 slug in his gut. I'll provide the slug and the trip—to hell." Mason felt for a chair and sat down. "Reckon I'm feeling generous. Tell Barkley that whatever he does, *don't* send anyone but one of Slade's riders.

After what happened today I believe Slade will kill anyone else that shows up out there."

"All right, you said 'first.' What else you want me to do?"

"Yeah, I did, didn't I? Well, next, go to the store and buy me about four pounds of salt, or Epsom salts, either one, it makes no difference. Then come back here. Don't tell anyone you've seen me except Barkley."

Murtry asked no more questions; he just put on his hat and slipped out the door.

When the door closed behind him, Mason took a bucket from a peg on the wall, filled it with water, and set it on the stove. He was glad for the cool evening that had caused Murtry to have a fire going. While the water heated, Mason carefully cleaned and oiled his guns, waiting for Murtry's return. Then he poured himself a cup of coffee from the pot Murtry always had on the stove.

Drinking, he checked the temperature of the water in the bucket several times. It finally heated such that he judged it acceptable for what he intended, and he plunged his right hand into it, still holding his coffee cup with the other.

The water finally got so hot he had to take it off the stove, still soaking his hand. Trying to flex his fingers, Mason thought he detected more movement in them. The heat seemed to be doing some good.

Hearing a noise, he drew his left handgun, leaving his right hand still submerged in the bucket. The door swung open, silently, and Murtry entered. Mason holstered his weapon.

Murtry nodded. "Done."

The one word told Mason as much as a dozen. So far his plan was going smoothly.

Murtry walked to the table and put a sack on it, then hung a gunnysack over the only window and lit a lantern. He reached to his hip pocket and pulled out a bottle of Barkley's best bourbon, looked questioningly at Mason, and when he nodded, poured a liberal amount of the sacred cache into a granite cup and handed it to him. Then he looked at Mason's hand in the bucket of water.

Eyebrows raised, Murtry's gaze locked with Mason's. "Reckoned when you wanted the salt, or salts, you'd done up an' got yourself hurt. Hold yore hand out here so's I can take a gander at it."

Mason held it, dripping, in front of Murtry's eyes.

Studying it a moment, Murtry pursed his lips and whistled, silently. "Broke?"

"Don't think so. I can still move my fingers a little."

Murtry nodded. "Good sign. Reckon you ain't much of a pistoleer right now, couldn't even trigger off a round onc't you got your iron clear of leather."

"Don't reckon I gotta give you much credit for noticing that, but you're right, I've tried and I can't even get my right handgun out of the holster."

"Well, shore hope you give yourself 'nuff time. Four days ain't much for *that* hand to git better."

"Didn't figure I could put it off longer, thought if I did it would give Slade a chance to get over the first shock of what we did to him, maybe get organized again, and start raising hell with the ranchers."

Murtry nodded. "Don't know what you done yet, so while I doctor on yore hand, tell me about it." He went to the table and took a large box of Epsom salts from the bag. "Figured this here was good fer a bullet hole or bruise. I'll put it in the water an' we'll soak that hand until you bed down, then I'll put some of my special horse linamint on it. That there linamint'll work while you git some sleep."

Murtry helped Mason with his hand until midnight, and while he did so, Mason told him of the Tomahawk Canyon fight.

"Well! Dagnab it, why didn't you let me he'p y'all out yonder? I kin shoot a rifle—an' reckon I coulda even throwed some of that there dynamite, bein's it was a straight-down sort of throw."

Mason brushed his hand through his hair. "Heck, Murtry, it wasn't your fight, and we had more than enough men already. I'll tell you one thing, though, if we'd needed you, I would surely have had someone burning leather to get you."

"Hot damn, just my luck. I done missed one a the best fights anybody ever had."

Mason soothed Murtry's hackles after a while, looked at the clock, and saw it was almost midnight. "It's been a long day, old-timer, think I'll spread my blanket in the hayloft and get some sleep."

"Nope. You're gonna sleep in my bed."

"Nope. I ain't," Mason mimicked. "You rub my hand down with some of that linamint you say is so good, and I'll go turn in."

"Oh, all right, but reckon I oughtta tell you, that there stuff burns like fire."

Mason nodded. "That's probably what makes it work so good."

"Well, goshding it, sure it is."

Murtry rubbed a liberal amount into Mason's hand, and on up to midway between his wrist and elbow. "There, that'll fix'er up fine. Now, let's turn in."

The salve was just as hot as Murtry had promised and smelled bad enough to bluff a skunk, but despite the heat and smell, Mason fell asleep almost as soon as he lay down.

A rooster crowed, a donkey brayed, and a mockingbird trilled its welcome to the new day. Mason opened his eyes a slit. It was not yet full daylight, but the smell of bacon frying and the aroma of fresh-brewed coffee made his taste buds tingle.

He threw back the blanket, rolled it, and climbed down the ladder, careful to protect his right hand. He was glad that Murtry had been thoughtful enough to have the pump put inside. It was in the back corner of the stable. Mason washed up and went in to find that Murtry had breakfast ready.

Together, they inspected his hand and saw noticeable improvement. Maybe, just maybe, Mason thought, it would be all right in the time he'd allowed.

The second morning it was better still. His fist would close almost all the way, and Mason was sure then that it would be in shape to draw and fire a handgun, perhaps not with his usual speed, but maybe good enough. Murtry had walked downtown to the post office, and to pick up on any talk about the canyon fight.

As soon as he walked in the door, Mason knew he had news.

"Hot dang it, b'lieve every dang body in town's abuzzin' 'bout that there shindig y'all done had out yonder." He sliced a fist through the air. "Jest me danged luck to be sittin' here while everything was happenin'. Didn't even feel like I could talk to anybody. They already knowed all about it."

Mason threw back his head and roared. When he could control his mirth, he looked at Murtry. "You act like everybody celebrated Christmas, and you slept through the whole thing."

"Well, dagnab it, that's the way I feel."

"Ah, c'mon, old-timer, the really big thing's gonna happen right here, and you're gonna be a part of it. Now tell me what you've heard that might let us know what Slade figures to do."

Murtry went to the stove and poured each of them a cup of coffee. Mason saw that it was as black as his socks after a three-month trail drive, but he took the cup offered him anyway.

"Tell you one thing," Murtry said, cocking his head to the side. "For two days now, Slade riders, or maybe I oughtta say, ex–Slade riders've been driftin' through town, headed outta the valley. Say they ain't never gonna face nobody what even looks like they know Cole. Say they believe ever' damned word they ever heard 'bout you." He sipped at the thick brew in his cup. "Whew, that's good. Thick 'nuff to git yore teeth into, ain't it?"

"Yeah, if it doesn't eat them off at the gums first."

Murtry checked the pail of water to see if it was still hot and made Mason put his hand back in it. "Main thing I found out is, Slade's only got about six or seven riders left. He give 'em a extra hunnerd dollars to stay with him."

Mason looked into his cup, then glanced at Murtry. "You know, old-timer, we're gonna win."

The last two of the four days passed. Mason looked at his hand, flexed his fingers, tried a practice draw, cock, and aim, and said, "Reckon Cole's ready for another gunfight."

"I shore ain't never seen nobody can beat what I jest seen you do with that .44."

Mason looked Murtry straight in the eyes. "Old-timer, when a man gets to thinking he's the best—that's when he's gonna find he isn't. But, reckon I'm as ready as I'll ever be. Keep the coffee hot. I don't think Slade'll be in town till 'bout noon. Come on down to Barkley's a little before then." He stood and walked slowly through the door.

Main Street spread before him. There were but three horses at the hitch rack in front of the saloon, and they didn't wear a

Box S brand. Slade was not yet in town. Mason walked to the bat-wing doors, pushed through them, and stepped quickly to the side. He leaned against the wall, waiting for his eyes to adjust to the darkened room. When he could see, he walked to the bar.

"I'll take the good stuff this time, Barkley." But Mason saw that Red had anticipated his preference, as he was already placing bottle and glass in front of him.

"How'd it go?" Barkley asked quietly. Mason knew he'd probably heard the story a hundred times, but wanted to hear it from the man who'd been there.

"Perfect. We didn't lose anybody. In fact, none of our people were hurt at all. Slade's through here in the valley."

"Careful, Mason. Neal Hamilton is sitting back there in the corner. He don't know yet how bad it was. Slade ain't been in town since the fight, and the townspeople haven't said anything to him that I know of. He knows something's wrong though, 'cause he's been sittin' back there sulking and drinking for three days now."

"Good. We won't tell him until after I face Slade. I want him out of the way first." He flexed his right hand under the overhang of the bar and wondered if he'd lost any speed, or accuracy.

"By the way, I told Martinez and some of the boys to come in and side me. I thought then that I'd have it to do the same day of the Tomahawk fight. You seen any of them?"

"Yeah, they come in after Murtry was in and told me what happened with your hand. I sent 'em back to your spread, told 'em to come in today. They wanted to see you. I told them, no, it'd be best if nobody went around where you were hiding until you said so. They went to the ranch."

Mason tossed down a shot of Barkley's bourbon, then looked at him. "I'm going outside and wait for Slade to show. Cover my back." Then he thought, not that it will make a hell of a lot of difference. If Hamilton wants to get in a shot, he'll do it.

He walked toward the door, then on impulse turned to Hamilton's table. "Slade's comin' in soon. I'm gonna give him his chance to show he's the great big man with a gun he thinks he is—you stay out of it. You'll have your chance later."

"Why not now?" Hamilton looked at him with a confident sneer.

"No. I'll take Slade first. Figure when I get rid of your partner, then the icing on the cake'll be you."

Hamilton frowned. "What do you mean, 'my partner'?"

Mason felt his eyes go flat and cold. "You deny that the two of you are working this scheme together? You loan money; he steals cows. Loans can't be paid off, and ultimately, you wind up with all the land in the valley."

"Damned right, I deny it. Who do you think you are, making accusations like that?"

"I'd say you and Slade were with the Murphy-Dolan gang, down Lincoln County way. They were running the same game there. You learned your lessons well, Hamilton."

Hamilton's eyes narrowed. "Let's say you got it figured right, *Mister* Mason, or whatever the hell your name is—my part of your make-believe game is legal. You figured out yet what you can do about that?"

Mason flashed him a cold smile, his eyes never leaving Hamilton's. "I know your henchmen have told you my name is Cole, so drop the pretense. And yes, I've figured what to do about you. You're a cold fish, Hamilton. You'd leave your partner to the hanging, or whatever we decide to do with him and his bunch, while you drag in the winnings."

Without looking at the bar, Mason signaled Barkley for a drink. "We could take you to court, Hamilton, but then we'd have to prove the partnership, and even if we could, it would take time—more time than we have."

Barkley brought his drink. Mason thanked him, taking the glass with his left hand.

"Well then, from where I stand, it looks like you and your trashy friends have just lost your last chip." Hamilton's smile was as cold as a mountain peak on a wintery morning. "What are you thinking of in the way of an alternative?"

Mason remained standing, aware that the few people in the saloon had moved quietly out of the line of fire. He moved a couple of steps to his left, making it a little harder for Hamilton to draw from his shoulder holster, bring his gun to bear, and fire. With Hamilton seated, Mason had the advantage and wasn't going to give it up.

"Gonna tell you something, Hamilton, figure you don't know yet, but four days ago we wiped Slade out. Most of his men have quit. He lost the herd, and he's been at the ranch since then, licking his wounds. You've lost your ace in the hole, Hamilton, so reckon instead of taking you on last, I'm gonna give you another couple of holes to breath through—right now."

Mason's hand was not as well as he wanted it to be, so he needed, and took, every advantage.

"Cash in your chips and get out of the game, or call my bluff." Mason's voice, soft as swan's down, dropped the gauntlet. "Now, Hamilton, right now. I'll not be looking over my shoulder for you—waiting for you to back-shoot me. Do it now, Hamilton."

Hamilton leaned back in his chair, hands fingering his lapels. He smiled, coldly. "I don't want trouble with—" His hand flashed inside his coat, brought out a snub-nosed .38, and fired. He missed. The bullet whined past Mason's ear, going over his shoulder.

Mason, his left hand holding the glass of whiskey, tossed it, glass and all, at Hamilton's face. His right hand a blur, he brought the muzzle of his .44 in line and thumbed off three shots.

Mason knew that Hamilton's second shot hit him somewhere, for a numbness covered his left side. He thumbed back the hammer for another shot, wondering what held Hamilton up. There were three black holes in the middle of his chest, each beginning to spread a red stain over his shirt.

There was such quiet in the saloon that Mason heard someone breathing across the room. Only two things moved: the drifting blanket of gunsmoke—and Hamilton.

He tried to train his gun on Mason again, but it seemed too heavy for him, and the hand holding it sank slowly to the table top. The veins stood out on his neck while he tried desperately to trigger another shot. He failed.

Eyes hate-filled, he stared at Mason. "You, bastard—you rotten bastard, you've killed me." His eyes opened wide, his hand slid from the table, his head lolled to the side, and he slumped down into the chair—dead.

From the time it started, to its end, went by so fast that Mason inhaled for the first time since letting his breath out for a steady draw.

Still staring at the dead man, he extracted spent shells and punched three fresh loads through the loading gate. Then, looking over his shoulder, he said, "Barkley, I could use another drink," and was surprised to see the redhead standing at his side holding a full glass of bourbon.

"Here, take this and sit down. You're hit."

"My side, I think, or maybe my leg, don't rightly know. The pain's not started yet."

Barkley placed the glass of bourbon on the table and helped Mason into the chair, then looked up at one of the small group of people who had gathered around. "Get *that*," he said, nodding at Hamilton's body, "out in the alley, and tell the undertaker he's got another customer." He turned his gaze on the next man. "You, Sanchez, go find the doc. Mason needs this hole plugged."

Mason now knew where he'd been hit; it wasn't hurting, but his pants were bloody about four inches above his knee, and the stain was spreading.

He pulled his bandana from around his neck and wrapped it around his leg, above the hole he now saw. He tied it tight and twisted it to stop the bleeding, then reached for the glass Barkley had brought him. Taking a mouthful, he swallowed, looked at Barkley, and smiled.

"It's downhill from here, Barkley. Hamilton was the hard one. If y'all will keep Slade's men off my back while I take care of him it'll—" The bat-wing doors burst open.

"Goshding it I done missed everything agin. Well, dadblame it, Mason—why in tarnation didn't you wait fer me to git here? I ain't seen one smidgen of what's happened."

Mason looked at Murtry, trying to hold in the laughter, but it wouldn't be held. He, Barkley, and the onlookers guffawed.

When he could control himself, Mason wiped tears from his eyes, drew his face into a sober look, and shook his head.

"Murtry, you know Hamilton hasn't cooperated with us on anything yet. He just wouldn't wait for you to get here."

"Aw, boy, quit joshin' me. I know you ain't gonna wait fer things, but . . . but, goshding it, how'm I gonna sit around and talk to people 'bout this here fight when I ain't seen nothing?"

"Tell you what, old-timer, I'll tell you my side of it—how I felt, what I did, how Hamilton lost—the whole thing. Then you'll know more than any who saw it."

Murtry wasn't easily mollified. "Well, reckon I'll have to take what I kin git."

The doors opened again, and Martinez and Mason's riders, all of them, rushed in.

"What happened?" Martinez said as he rushed to Mason's side.

"I already tangled with Hamilton—now for Slade. He'll be here sometime today. All I want you men to do is don't let anybody get at my back."

Martinez glanced at Mason's leg. "Anybody go for the doc?"

Mason nodded. "He'll be here soon if he's in town; if not, I'll wrap it with something until after we're through with Slade."

"All right. I'll get the men, how do you say eet, positioned? Sí, I'll get them positioned."

"I'll be out shortly." Mason watched Martinez and his crew leave, then looked at his leg and saw that the bleeding had stopped. "Barkley, you got a clean bar towel? I'll just wrap it around the hole and take care of what's coming. If the doc shows up, tell 'im I'll see him later."

Slowly, savoring the taste of it, Mason sipped his drink, letting Barkley tie the bar towel around his leg while he drank. When Barkley had finished, Mason stood and limped toward the door.

He pushed the doors open and let them swing closed as he limped through. He stepped to the side as soon as they closed. His penetrating gaze searched out every nook that might hide an enemy.

He glanced at the roof line of each building and saw that Martinez, Brody, and Brannigan had gotten in position. A rifle barrel poked from behind every false front. He frowned. There were a lot more guns showing than his men would have. He wondered where the rest of the guns had come from and hoped the ranchers stayed out of it, as he'd told them to do.

He saw Martinez climb to the peak of the hotel roof—it was the tallest building in town—and look off to the north and point, then hold up eight fingers. Slade was on his way in with eight men, more than Mason had thought would stay with him.

"At least we're not outnumbered," he reflected. Then he said under his breath, "It will soon be over—one way or another."

He stood, a tall lonely figure, in the middle of the street, waiting for the crash of gunfire that would signal the end of the trail for some, and hopefully, a bright new beginning for others. He knew the kind of figure he made standing there. He'd seen too many others in similar situations.

He did not have long to wait. Slade and his riders topped the hill and rode slowly toward him. He watched until they were within about forty feet, all riding abreast except Slade, who was out ahead of them a few feet. He held up his left hand.

"You've come far enough, Slade." His voice was quiet, but the town seemed to be holding its breath. It was so quiet that those on horseback, and on the roofs, could hear his words.

"This town is closed to you. You and your men ride out— out of the valley—and live. If you stay here, we'll hang you."

"Who the hell do you think you are? I came in here to see Hamilton, my banker. Now get the hell out of my way or I'll blow you out," Slade threatened, and swung down from his mount.

"You men," Mason bit off his words, "don't make any foolish moves. There are a dozen rifles pointed at you."

He saw them cast furtive glances around; then almost as one they folded their hands on their pommels. Seeing them heed his warning, Mason hoped that maybe this thing could end with little killing.

"It looks like it comes down to you and me, Slade, and you aren't half the man with a gun you think you are. Hamilton was better'n you, but found he wasn't good enough. He learned that lesson the hard way. I decorated his shirtfront with three new holes. They were a mite large for buttons, but then he wasn't in a position to be choosey."

He saw an uncertain flicker in the flat sheen of Slade's eyes, and maybe even a little fear. He hoped he was right. If he could rattle Slade enough, then maybe even with his hand still slightly swollen, he could get off the best shot.

With a careful, measured step toward Slade, Mason continued, "Now, Slade, I'm gonna send you down that last, long, lonely trail." He took another step. "You're through here, Slade, here and anywhere else you go. Whenever you feel lucky, draw, but you've never really been that good with a gun, have you, Slade?"

Mason had forgotten his hand; he had reverted to the primitive man that is in all of us. He wanted to kill—this gutless monster in front of him had ridden over helpless men, women, and children. He continued his slow, measured steps.

Slade backed up a step. Mason took two, and then saw raw, shameless fear explode across Slade's face, his hands held wide of his guns.

"Yeah, I'm gonna kill you first, and then I'm gonna kill that pinch-faced bastard you call a brother." He took another step. "C'mon, Tom Slade, get off your horse. Come down here with your brother so I can show you the same hospitality I'm showing him. I'll give you both first draw."

He was aware that Tom Slade had moved his hands from the pommel to hold them above his head. "I don't want any part of this. It's you an' Bart. I never done nothin to you, Cole," he whined.

"So, it's not even going to be much of a fight." Mason took another step. He was within ten feet of Slade. He saw sweat running down Bart's face, and it was a cool day.

Bart's lower lip began to quiver. Mason closed the last few feet between them.

"Drop your gunbelt, and I hope you make a move toward your gun. Drop it, big bad man." Mason continued to taunt him, his voice soft, even, void of expression.

Slade's hands moved slowly, carefully, toward the buckle of his gunbelt, then trembled violently as they fumbled with the buckle. He let belt and gun drop, half-circling his feet.

Mason reached out and deliberately slapped Bart Slade—one cheek and then the other.

"You're gonna leave this town, and this valley. You're not going to your ranch for any gear. Leave your horse here. All you're leaving with is the clothes on your back. But first, you're gonna come in Barkley's place and sign over your cattle and ranch to the ranchers. Now, *move*."

Mason was almost sick to his stomach. The sickness was not from what he'd just done. He'd destroyed a man, more completely than simply blowing him to hell. But he was sick that there were men, breathing the same air that he breathed, as gutless as this worthless excuse standing in front of him.

The Slade men looked contemptuously at their boss, then reined their horses around to leave. One of them stopped and turned back.

"You're everything they said you were, Cole. This is your town, and your valley; you'll have no more trouble here—not from me anyway." He pulled his horse around and followed those he'd ridden with for so long.

Mason felt empty, drained. When Slade signed the papers, it would all be over.

"C'mon inside, the drinks're on the house—for the whole damned town if they want them," Barkley roared.

Mason had started to follow him in when a thin, scared voice came from behind.

"Can a lady come in for a drink?"

He spun toward the voice, knowing it to be Laura's.

"What in the *hell* are you doing here? Why aren't you at the ranch?"

Her chin tilted stubbornly. "I'm going inside and have a drink with you whether you like it or not; then I'll tell you why I'm not at the ranch."

Mason looked at her a moment, ashamed he'd spoken to her as he had, taking his nerves out on her. Then pride swelled his throat almost shut. He took her arm. "Let's go have that drink, little one. I'm sorry I spoke as I did."

The town came alive around them. As Mason pushed into the saloon he saw men—and women—sliding down roofs to ladders and heading toward him. All carried rifles.

He escorted Laura into Barkley's place, walked to a table, and seated her. It was the table closest to the bar. Her eyes traveled in wonder down its shiny length. Mason realized she'd never seen the inside of a saloon before.

"Stay where you are while I help Slade make us all a few cows and one ranch better off."

Mason prodded Slade to a back table, looked over his shoulder at Barkley, and said, "Get the lawyer. We've a little business to transact."

The lawyer came and went. All of Slade's holdings were then legally the property of the valley ranchers. Mason made sure Slade was stripped of everything except the clothes he wore, then limped to the edge of town with him. Slade's holdings would be divided later.

"Slade, don't ever come back this way—not ever again. And if I hear of you teaming with another like Hamilton, and trying to run the same deal on others, I'll hunt you down, then I'll gut-shoot you and stand by while you die. Now—get gone."

Mason stood, watching, until Slade topped the rise at the south end of town. He watched him walk, head bent, shoulders bowed, but Mason could muster no sympathy for him. He turned toward the saloon.

People started to trickle in—men and women from town, women from the ranches, along with their older kids, some as young as twelve years.

Mason knew that none of these people had ever been in a saloon before. He also knew that they had been the ones holding the rifles he'd seen sticking around the false fronts of the town's stores. They gathered around him, and standing off to one side were Bryson and Sisson.

"What are you two doing here?" he growled.

"The same thing every other man, woman, and child in this valley is doing," Bryson growled back. "We were hoping to keep our leading citizen, and my future son-in-law, from gittin' his self blowed to hell."

Knowing they could have only prevented Slade's men from getting in the fight didn't lessen Mason's admiration, and gratitude. The code of the West would not allow them to interfere in his confrontation with Slade, but had they not been where they were, when he needed them, he would now be dead. He might have gotten Slade—and maybe one or two of his men—but without the townspeople and ranchers, Slade's men would have gotten him before it was over.

He started to tell them, then settled back in his chair.

He didn't have to tell them that never again would they have to bow their heads to anyone. Today they'd earned the right to hold their heads high in any company.

He twisted in his chair. "Brody, if you will, I want you to stay on and ramrod the Larsen place. Pa will only come and go as he wishes, but I want you to run it, and you, Martinez, I've a special place picked out for my home. I want you to help me build it, and we'll build yours close by. Brannigan, Bryson needs you, but if you ever want a permanent home, you have one with me." He looked at Murtry and Barkley. "Thanks for my life, friends."

They fidgeted uncomfortably. Barkley's face lit up to about the same color as his hair.

"I ain't much at talkin'," he said, "but you gave us our life. You taught us, or at least made us realize again, that life without freedom is worse than death." He lifted his glass. "Thanks to *you*, my friend."

Mason twisted his head and looked at Laura. "Now, young lady, you gonna tell me why you're here in town?"

Her chin tilted, stubbornly, again. "I'm where I belong, where I'll be the rest of my life—with my man."

He opened his arms and she came into them.

"Let's go home, young'un." He leaned over and kissed her. He didn't care if the whole town saw it.

FURY KNEW SOMETHING was wrong long before he saw the wagon train spread out, unmoving, across the plains in front of him.

From miles away, he had noticed the cloud of dust kicked up by the hooves of the mules and oxen pulling the wagons. Then he had seen that tan-colored pall stop and gradually be blown away by the ceaseless prairie wind.

It was the middle of the afternoon, much too early for a wagon train to be stopping for the day. Now, as Fury topped a small, grass-covered ridge and saw the motionless wagons about half a mile away, he wondered just what kind of damn fool was in charge of the train.

Stopping out in the open without even forming into a circle was like issuing an invitation to the Sioux, the Cheyenne, or the Pawnee. War parties roamed these plains all the time just looking for a situation as tempting as this one.

Fury reined in, leaned forward in his saddle, and thought about it. Nothing said he had to go help those pilgrims. They might not even want his help. But from the looks of things, they needed his help, whether they wanted it or not.

He heeled the rangy lineback dun into a trot toward the wagons. As he approached, he saw figures scurrying back and forth around the canvas-topped vehicles. Looked sort of like an anthill after someone stomped it.

Fury pulled the dun to a stop about twenty feet from the lead wagon. Near it a man was stretched out on the ground with so many men and women gathered around him that Fury could only catch a glimpse of him through the crowd. When some of the men turned to look at him, Fury said, "Howdy. Thought it looked like you were having trouble."

175

"Damn right, mister," one of the pilgrims snapped. "And if you're of a mind to give us more, I'd advise against it."

Fury crossed his hands on the saddlehorn and shifted in the saddle, easing his tired muscles. "I'm not looking to cause trouble for anybody," he said mildly.

He supposed he might appear a little threatening to a bunch of immigrants who until now had never been any farther west than the Mississippi. Several days had passed since his face had known the touch of the razor, and his rough-hewn features could be a little intimidating even without the beard stubble. Besides that, he was well armed with a Colt's Third Model Dragoon pistol holstered on his right hip, a Bowie knife sheathed on his left, and a Sharps carbine in the saddleboot under his right thigh. And he had the look of a man who knew how to use all three weapons.

A husky, broad-shouldered six-footer, John Fury's height was apparent even on horseback. He wore a broad-brimmed, flat-crowned black hat, a blue work shirt, and fringed buckskin pants that were tucked into high-topped black boots. As he swung down from the saddle, a man's voice, husky with strain, called out, "Who's that? Who are you?"

The crowd parted, and Fury got a better look at the figure on the ground. It was obvious that he was the one who had spoken. There was blood on the man's face, and from the twisted look of him as he lay on the ground, he was busted up badly inside.

Fury let the dun's reins trail on the ground, confident that the horse wouldn't go anywhere. He walked over to the injured man and crouched beside him. "Name's John Fury," he said.

The man's breath hissed between his teeth, whether in pain or surprise Fury couldn't have said. "Fury? I heard of you."

Fury just nodded. Quite a few people reacted that way when they heard his name.

"I'm . . . Leander Crofton. Wagonmaster of . . . this here train." The man struggled to speak. He appeared to be in his fifties and had a short, grizzled beard and the leathery skin of a man who had spent nearly his whole life outdoors. His pale blue eyes were narrowed in a permanent squint.

"What happened to you?" Fury asked.

"It was a terrible accident— " began one of the men standing nearby, but he fell silent when Fury cast a hard glance at him.

Fury had asked Crofton, and that was who he looked toward for the answer.

Crofton smiled a little, even though it cost him an effort. "Pulled a damn fool stunt," he said. "Horse nearly stepped on a rattler, and I let it rear up and get away from me. Never figured the critter'd spook so easy." The wagonmaster paused to draw a breath. The air rattled in his throat and chest. "Tossed me off and stomped all over me. Not the first time I been stepped on by a horse, but then a couple of the oxen pullin' the lead wagon got me, too, 'fore the driver could get 'em stopped."

"God forgive me, I . . . I am so sorry." The words came in a tortured voice from a small man with dark curly hair and a beard. He was looking down at Crofton with lines of misery etched onto his face.

"Wasn't your fault, Leo," Crofton said. "Just . . . bad luck."

Fury had seen men before who had been trampled by horses. Crofton was in a bad way, and Fury could tell by the look in the man's eyes that Crofton was well aware of it. The wagonmaster's chances were pretty slim.

"Mind if I look you over?" Fury asked. Maybe he could do something to make Crofton's passing a little easier, anyway.

One of the other men spoke before Crofton had a chance to answer. "Are you a doctor, sir?" he asked.

Fury glanced up at him, saw a slender, middle-aged man with iron-gray hair. "No, but I've patched up quite a few hurt men in my time."

"Well, I am a doctor," the gray-haired man said. "And I'd appreciate it if you wouldn't try to move or examine Mr. Crofton. I've already done that, and I've given him some laudanum to ease the pain."

Fury nodded. He had been about to suggest a shot of whiskey, but the laudanum would probably work better.

Crofton's voice was already slower and more drowsy from the drug as he said, "Fury . . ."

"Right here."

"I got to be sure about something . . . You said your name was . . . John Fury."

"That's right."

"The same John Fury who . . . rode with Fremont and Kit Carson?"

"I know them," Fury said simply.

"And had a run-in with Cougar Johnson in Santa Fe?"

"Yes."

"Traded slugs with Hemp Collier in San Antone last year?"

"He started the fight, didn't give me much choice but to finish it."

"Thought so." Crofton's hand lifted and clutched weakly at Fury's sleeve. "You got to . . . make me a promise."

Fury didn't like the sound of that. Promises made to dying men usually led to a hell of a lot of trouble.

Crofton went on, "You got to give me . . . your word . . . that you'll take these folks through . . . to where they're goin'."

"I'm no wagonmaster," Fury said.

"You know the frontier," Crofton insisted. Anger gave him strength, made him rally enough to lift his head from the ground and glare at Fury. "You can get 'em through. I know you can."

"Don't excite him," warned the gray-haired doctor.

"Why the hell not?" Fury snapped, glancing up at the physician. He noticed now that the man had his arm around the shoulders of a pretty red-headed girl in her teens, probably his daughter. He went on, "What harm's it going to do?"

The girl exclaimed, "Oh! How can you be so . . . so callous?"

Crofton said, "Fury's just bein' practical, Carrie. He knows we got to . . . got to hash this out now. Only chance we'll get." He looked at Fury again. "I can't make you promise, but it . . . it'd sure set my mind at ease while I'm passin' over if I knew you'd take care of these folks."

Fury sighed. It was rare for him to promise anything to anybody. Giving your word was a quick way of getting in over your head in somebody else's problems. But Crofton was dying, and even though they had never crossed paths before, Fury recognized in the old man a fellow Westerner.

"All right," he said.

A little shudder ran through Crofton's battered body, and he rested his head back against the grassy ground. "Thanks," he said, the word gusting out of him along with a ragged breath.

"Where are you headed?" Fury figured the immigrants could tell him, but he wanted to hear the destination from Crofton.

"Colorado Territory . . . Folks figure to start 'em a town . . . somewhere on the South Platte. Won't be hard for you to find . . . a good place."

No, it wouldn't, Fury thought. No wagon train journey could be called easy, but at least this one wouldn't have to deal with crossing mountains, just prairie.

Prairie filled with savages and outlaws, that is.

A grim smile plucked at Fury's mouth as that thought crossed his mind. "Anything else you need to tell me?" he asked Crofton.

The wagonmaster shook his head and let his eyelids slide closed. "Nope. Figger I'll rest a spell now. We can talk again later."

"Sure," Fury said softly, knowing that in all likelihood, Leander Crofton would never wake up from this rest.

Less than a minute later, Crofton coughed suddenly, a wracking sound. His head twisted to the side, and blood welled for a few seconds from the corner of his mouth. Fury heard some of the women in the crowd cry out and turn away, and he suspected some of the men did, too.

"Well, that's all," he said, straightening easily from his kneeling position beside Crofton's body. He looked at the doctor. The red-headed teenager had her face pressed to the front of her father's shirt and her shoulders were shaking with sobs. She wasn't the only one crying, and even the ones who were dry-eyed still looked plenty grim.

"We'll have a funeral service as soon as a grave is dug," said the doctor. "Then I suppose we'll be moving on. You should know, Mr. . . . Fury, was it? You should know that none of us will hold you to that promise you made to Mr. Crofton."

Fury shrugged. "Didn't ask if you intended to or not. I'm the one who made the promise. Reckon I'll keep it."

He saw surprise on some of the faces watching him. All of these travelers had probably figured him for some sort of drifter. Well, that was fair enough. Drifting was what he did best.

But that didn't mean he was a man who ignored promises. He had given his word, and there was no way he could back out now.

He met the startled stare of the doctor and went on, "Who's the captain here? You?"

"No, I . . . You see, we hadn't gotten around to electing a captain yet. We only left Independence a couple of weeks ago, and we were all happy with the leadership of Mr. Crofton. We didn't see the need to select a captain."

Crofton should have insisted on it, Fury thought with a grimace. You never could tell when trouble would pop up. Crofton's body lying on the ground was grisly proof of that.

Fury looked around at the crowd. From the number of people standing there, he figured most of the wagons in the train were at least represented in this gathering. Lifting his voice, he said, "You all heard what Crofton asked me to do. I gave him my word I'd take over this wagon train and get it on through to Colorado Territory. Anybody got any objection to that?"

His gaze moved over the faces of the men and women who were standing and looking silently back at him. The silence was awkward and heavy. No one was objecting, but Fury could tell they weren't too happy with this unexpected turn of events.

Well, he thought, when he had rolled out of his soogans that morning, he hadn't expected to be in charge of a wagon train full of strangers before the day was over.

The gray-haired doctor was the first one to find his voice. "We can't speak for everyone on the train, Mr. Fury," he said. "But I don't know you, sir, and I have some reservations about turning over the welfare of my daughter and myself to a total stranger."

Several others in the crowd nodded in agreement with the sentiment expressed by the physician.

"Crofton knew me."

"He knew you to have a reputation as some sort of gunman!"

Fury took a deep breath and wished to hell he had come along after Crofton was already dead. Then he wouldn't be saddled with a pledge to take care of these people.

"I'm not wanted by the law," he said. "That's more than a lot of men out here on the frontier can say, especially those who have been here for as long as I have. Like I said, I'm not looking to cause trouble. I was riding along and minding my own business when I came across you people. There's too many of you for me to fight. You want to start out toward Colorado on your own, I can't stop you. But you're going to have to learn a hell of a lot in a hurry."

"What do you mean by that?"

Fury smiled grimly. "For one thing, if you stop spread out like this, you're making a target of yourselves for every Indian in these parts who wants a few fresh scalps for his lodge." He looked pointedly at the long red hair of the doctor's daughter. Carrie—that was what Crofton had called her, Fury remembered.

Her father paled a little, and another man said, "I didn't think there was any Indians this far east." Other murmurs of concern came from the crowd.

Fury knew he had gotten through to them. But before any of them had a chance to say that he should honor his promise to Crofton and take over, the sound of hoofbeats made him turn quickly.

A man was riding hard toward the wagon train from the west, leaning over the neck of his horse and urging it on to greater speed. The brim of his hat was blown back by the wind of his passage, and Fury saw anxious, dark brown features underneath it. The newcomer galloped up to the crowd gathered next to the lead wagon, hauled his lathered mount to a halt, and dropped lithely from the saddle. His eyes went wide with shock when he saw Crofton's body on the ground, and then his gaze flicked to Fury.

"You son of a bitch!" he howled.

And his hand darted toward the gun holstered on his hip.

If you enjoyed this book, subscribe now and get...

TWO FREE

A $7.00 VALUE—

If you would like to read more of the very best, most exciting, adventurous, action-packed Westerns being published today, you'll want to subscribe to True Value's Western Home Subscription Service.

Each month the editors of True Value will select the 6 very best Westerns from America's leading publishers for special readers like you. You'll be able to preview these new titles as soon as they are published, *FREE* for ten days with no obligation!

TWO FREE BOOKS

When you subscribe, we'll send you your first month's shipment of the newest and best 6 Westerns for you to preview. With your first shipment, two of these books will be yours as our introductory gift to you absolutely *FREE* (a $7.00 value), regardless of what you decide to do. If

you like them, as much as we think you will, keep all six books but pay for just 4 at the low subscriber rate of just $2.75 each. If you decide to return them, keep 2 of the titles as our gift. No obligation.

Special Subscriber Savings

When you become a True Value subscriber you'll save money several ways. First, all regular monthly selections will be billed at the low subscriber price of just $2.75 each. That's at least a savings of $4.50 each month below the publishers price. Second, there is never any shipping, handling or other hidden charges—*Free home delivery*. What's more there is no minimum number of books you must buy, you may return any selection for full credit and you can cancel your subscription at any time. A TRUE VALUE!

WESTERNS!

NO OBLIGATION

Mail the coupon below

To start your subscription and receive 2 FREE WESTERNS, fill out the coupon below and mail it today. We'll send your first shipment which includes 2 FREE BOOKS as soon as we receive it.

Mail To: **True Value Home Subscription Services, Inc. P.O. Box 5235 120 Brighton Road, Clifton, New Jersey 07015-5235**

YES! I want to start reviewing the very best Westerns being published today. Send me my first shipment of 6 Westerns for me to preview FREE for 10 days. If I decide to keep them, I'll pay for just 4 of the books at the low subscriber price of $2.75 each; a total $11.00 (a $21.00 value). Then each month I'll receive the 6 newest and best Westerns to preview Free for 10 days. If I'm not satisfied I may return them within 10 days and owe nothing. Otherwise I'll be billed at the special low subscriber rate of $2.75 each; a total of $16.50 (at least a $21.00 value) and save $4.50 off the publishers price. There are never any shipping, handling or other hidden charges. I understand I am under no obligation to purchase any number of books and I can cancel my subscription at any time, no questions asked. In any case the 2 FREE books are mine to keep.

Name _____

Street Address _____ Apt. No. _____

City _____ State _____ Zip Code _____

Telephone _____

Signature _____
(if under 18 parent or guardian must sign)

10879

Terms and prices subject to change. Orders subject to acceptance by True Value Home Subscription Services, Inc.